Angel's Retreat

by

Carol Marlene Smith

ACKNOWLEDGMENTS

Cover photo by Broderick Mossman

Note from Author: This novel is written in Canadian/British English

ISBN: 1481028650
ISBN-13: 978-1481028653

Books by Carol Marlene Smith

Angel's Blessing

Heart of Winter

Jewell

Who Wants to Murder a Millionaire?

1964: Chasing A Dream

Facing Reality

Angel's Retreat

Death and Deceit

PROLOGUE

Lots of events occurred in August. It was Aunt May's birthday month, the month that Angel and Jake got married and now it was the birth month of Angel and Jake's new daughter.

"When is that baby gonna be born anyway, Aunt May?" Nine-year-old Rachael sat squirming across from her great aunt in the hospital waiting room.

"When *that* baby is ready, I suppose. Don't be so impatient. Here, take this five dollar bill to the cafeteria and get us both a drink. I'll have tea."

Rachael bounded down from her chair and took off to the cafeteria. Just as Rachael rounded the corner and out of sight, Jake appeared from the delivery room. "Things are looking up, May, shouldn't be long now."

"Rachael was getting antsy so I sent her to the cafeteria for something to do."

Jake laughed. "I'd love to stay and chat, May, but Angel needs me in there."

"That baby will be born whether you're there or not, Jake Jordan. But yes, you should scoot back in there and give Angel some support at least."

"What does that mean?"

May grinned. "Men," she said, "are mostly in the way when it comes to birthing, but women have them around so they feel useful."

Jake gave her a look and pushed the delivery room door open, disappearing inside. He was shocked to see the beehive of activity going on. When he'd left a couple of minutes earlier, all was calm, now it looked like things were happening.

Jake rushed to the head of Angel's bed and grabbed her hand. "I'm here, Angel. Just listen to the doctor and everything will be okay."

Angel could feel Jake's hand trembling, even though the other feelings, pain mostly, going through her were overwhelming his shaking hand. She wanted to speak to Jake to reassure him that yes, everything would be okay, but she was afraid. What if everything wasn't okay?

"Push, Angel, push." The doctor's voice was demanding and Angel turned her attention to the task at hand. With one great, giant contraction eroding her stomach, she heard the words, "She's crowning." Then she heard, "Looks like a ten. Look at that red hair!" Angel opened her eyes, as the doctor stood to her left holding a little bundle that was screaming at the top of her lungs. "I think she has a red-head's temper also." The doctor laughed.

She handed Angel the baby and Angel's arms trembled, as she looked at her tiny daughter. Tears rolled down her cheeks and she turned to Jake.

"Isn't she the most precious, beautiful thing?"

Jake's eyes were also filled to the brim and overflowing. Angel passed the baby to Jake and he curled his arms around her. "She certainly is," he marvelled.

A nurse stood behind Jake. "I have to take her for a bit for her APGAR testing. I won't be long."

Angel lay back on the bed and closed her eyes again, thankful and grateful that her little daughter was finally here.

"Angel, do you feel okay?"

Angel opened her eyes and looked at Jake, who wore an apprehensive face. "I feel fine, Jake." She laid her hand on his. "Why don't you go out and tell the others about the baby?"

Jake turned quickly to leave then hesitated and turned back. He bent to give Angel a kiss. "Thank you for a lovely daughter. I love you."

"I love you too, now go."

****

A couple of hours later, Angel was settled in her hospital room nursing her newly born baby girl.

"Why does she look so wrinkly?" Rachael wanted to know.

Angel smiled at Rachael. "She's brand new that's why. She needs to grow into her skin."

"Eeww," Rachael remarked.

"You probably looked just as wrinkled, young lady when you were born," Aunt May informed her.

"Well, I think she's just beautiful," Jake's sister, Tanya announced. "She's a combination of both Jake and Angel. Look at those eyes…that's Jake, and that hair is definitely Angel."

There was laughter in the room and nine-year-old Rachael sang while dancing around the room, "She's going to be a red head…she's going to be a red head."

"Okay, blondie," Jake intervened. "Aunt Tanya has volunteered to take you home to her place for the night. What do you think about that?"

"Great. I love going to Aunt Tanya's." She looked up at Tanya. "Can I use your computer?"

"Come on," Tanya said. "We'll talk about that in the car."

"Are you coming, May?" Tanya wanted to know.

May drew close to Angel's bedside and said, "Not until I know what this child is going to be called. These two have kept it a secret long enough, so let's hear it."

Angel looked at Jake and they both grinned. Jake announced, "Mae

2

Marjorie. I just wish that Mom and Dad could have been here, but they're always gallivanting off somewhere since they retired."

"I know your mother will be happy that we named the baby after her. What do you think, May, are you happy to have the first name, or should we change it to Marjorie Mae?" Angel asked, with a glint in her eye.

May grinned from ear to ear, "I'd say it's quite a beautiful name, just the way it is. I hope she can live up to it."

"With that red hair, I'm sure she will live up to it, May," Tanya said.

After all had left the room and there was only Jake at her bedside, Angel heaved a long sigh.

"What was that for?" Jake questioned.

"Relief."

"We have two daughters now. Isn't that wonderful?"

"Yes, Jake, it's the most wonderful thing in the world."

CHAPTER ONE
Summer 2010

Angel trembled, as if an earthquake had just occurred, then all the lights went out.

Rachael came into the living room in a rush as usual. "Mom, my car won't start, is it okay if I borrow yours tonight? I have a…"

Her voice caught in her throat when she saw Angel sprawled on the carpet, the phone two feet from her, blaring out a busy signal.

"Mom!" Rachael finally found her voice. She bent towards Angel and her knees buckled as she knelt before her, tapping her lightly on the cheek and repeating her name. But Angel was out cold.

The only other person in the house was nine-year-old Mae, and Rachael didn't want her to see their mother in this condition. She grabbed the phone and punched in 911. By the time someone answered, Angel was stirring.

"Never mind," Rachael yelled into the phone. "My mother fainted but she's coming around now so I'm sorry to have called you. I will, yes I will. If she needs further attention I'll call back. Thank you."

Dropping the phone back onto the carpet, Rachael gave her full attention to a moaning Angel. "Mom, what happened? Are you okay?"

Angel stared up at her, but she couldn't speak, nor could she let herself believe the words she had heard on the phone. Instead she closed her eyes and screamed, "NO!"

"No? No, you're not all right? What's wrong? Do you hurt somewhere? Were you dizzy? Did you break anything?"

Rachael proceeded to feel Angel's arms and legs to see if anything might be broken. Although she was no nurse, she did have some idea about broken bones; after all she was a veterinarian student. Animals and people were not all that different.

Angel seemed to be okay physically. "Mom, snap out of it! What's wrong?"

"Jake…your father…he's…he's…." Angel curled up in a ball and covered her face with her hands.

"Who was on the phone?" Rachael prodded.

"I don't know." Angel began to rock gently, moaning to herself.

"What do you mean, you don't know? Mom, for God's sake tell me what's wrong!"

"Some associate…he said he was in the car with Jake. He's at the hospital."

"Dad's at the hospital?"

"No, the other guy is. Your dad—"

"Mom, where is Dad?" By now Rachael was getting the creeps. She was hot, she was cold, she shivered and she couldn't control the trembles. If her dad was not at the hospital and the other guy was, and he was calling Angel to say…what?

"Mom, look at me, look…at…me!" Rachael pulled Angel's hands away from her face and made her mother look at her. "Now tell me what he said."

Angel's eyes were scary, they looked beyond frightened. What Rachael saw was horror. "Your dad was in a car crash."

Rachael covered her ears. She did not want to hear anymore. But what she heard was too loud to ignore.

"He's dead!" Angel screamed again and rolled to her feet running from the room. The sounds that she heard coming from her own insides were hardly human. She needed to get away.

Rachael stared after her mother, she could not breathe, her lungs felt as if they had collapsed. She tried to stand but her legs would not support her. She crumbled to the floor. This could not be happening. Her throat hurt as if she had just run a long way. Suddenly she gasped and drew in a long breath. She sat listening. She had heard something, a low cry or whine.

She thought of Mae. Where was Mae? She had to find her before her mom did. She didn't know which way to turn, what to do. She wanted to call someone, but who? Aunt Tanya…she'd know what to do. Rachael's fingers trembled as she called the number but got a voice message. She wanted to run…somewhere, anywhere that she didn't have to face what was going on here.

She took another long breath and told herself she had to calm down. Someone in this house had to make sense. She picked up the phone and checked for the last incoming number. She called it.

"Hello."

"Who is this?" Rachael asked.

"Who is this?"

"It's Rachael Jordan. Do you know my dad?"

There was a pause then, "Rachael, I shouldn't be talking to you right now. I called your mother—"

"My mother's a little crazy right now. I can't make sense of anything she says. So, mister who-ever-you-are, you had better tell me what's going on."

He sighed. "Okay. Your dad didn't make it. A car came out of no where and over to our side. It was going like hell. By the time Jake saw it…it was too late to do anything. It hit us side on, your dad's side."

Rachael dropped the phone. She ran…out of the room, out of the house, out of sight. She went to her cubby hole. It was where she had always gone when things were bad, or when she wanted privacy. Her dad had made it for her after he and Angel had married. She didn't always go there when things were bad; she went there when things were good too. She went there whenever she wanted, she was there now.

She had left a message with her aunt to come quickly, something was horribly wrong. She had not wanted to scare her aunt but this was an emergency, and although she was nineteen and supposed to be an adult, she didn't know what to do.

Well, hiding in her cubby hole was not going to be the answer. Although it was where she wanted to stay…forever, she knew that Mae was in the house, and she had no idea where her mom was. If she was screaming somewhere then poor little Mae was going to be terrified.

Rachael hurried back to the house. She bounded up the stairs and into Mae's room. She didn't see Mae.

"Mae? Are you here?"

Rachael heard a whimper and knelt down to pull the bed skirt aside. "Mae, come out of there." Mae crawled out slowly, still whimpering.

Rachael held Mae in her arms. "Have you heard?"

"I heard Mommy screaming and it scared me. What's wrong with Mommy, Rachael?"

"Mom will be fine, Mae. But there's something I have to tell you. Dad was in a car accident. He…he…died."

It was not what Rachael expected to happen next. The little girl did not cry, she did not yell or scream or take a fit. She lay stone still against Rachael's chest, her head in the cradle of Rachael's shoulder and neck.

In a way Rachael was relieved. She knew it might be harmful to Mae, but everyone grieves in their own way. What should she do now? She couldn't leave her sister alone, but where was their mother?

"Rachael? You up there? What's wrong?"

Rachael let a breath out. It was her Aunt Tanya. She jumped up, pulling Mae with her. "Sit on the bed. I'll be right back."

Rachael ran down the stairs and straight into her Aunt Tanya's arms. "It's horrible, Aunt Tanya. My dad is dead. A car hit him."

Tanya enfolded Rachael in her arms. Through tears that now seemed like they were trying to drown her, Rachael told all to her Aunt Tanya.

Tanya suddenly pulled from Rachael. "Where's Angel? And where's Mae?"

"Mae's in her room just sitting there. She knows. She's not crying. She scares me. I…I don't know where Mom is. She got the call and she ran out of the living room screaming like she had gone mad."

****

Tanya turned in a circle at the bottom of the stairs with her hand over her mouth, thinking. She didn't know what to do next. Mae was upstairs in shock. Rachael was acting sort of in control, but really that seemed weird too. And Lord only knew where Angel was, probably rolled up in a ball somewhere.

Tanya knew that Jake and the children were Angel's life. What would she ever do without him? In fact, what would she, herself, do without her brother, who'd always been there for her, whenever she needed him?

Yes, Jake had been one of a kind when it came to men. Understanding, straightforward, trustworthy, suddenly she could hear the eulogy with his friends stating many of those very qualities. Tanya knew it was no time for her to be thinking of the past or the future. She was now placed in a position that no one wanted to be in, but it was up to her to be the strength in this family now.

Putting her own feelings aside, she knew she had to find Angel. Tanya called up the stairs to Rachael who came to the top of the stairs. "I want you to stay with Mae, get her interested in something, drawing, colouring, or whatever you can think of."

It was a heavy burden to ask of Rachael, who had just lost her beloved father who meant everything to her, but Tanya didn't know what else to do. She was flying here, hoping not to fall. Once Tanya had established where Rachael and Mae would be, she headed outside to look for Angel and noticed that Angel's car was gone.

"Oh, my God," she mumbled. Where would she go? Where else but to her Aunt May's? Hoping she was right, Tanya got in her own car and drove to May's house.

Driving towards the manor, Tanya thought of May's ninetieth birthday. As usual a big celebration had taken place at Angel and Jake's house. Jake so loved Angel's aunt, like she was his own. And after marrying Angel, May did become his aunt.

She pulled up into the manor yard relieved to see Angel's car there, but hesitant to go inside. Instead she took a walk around the property to see if Angel and May might be outside.

Walking through the orchard Tanya spied Angel, but she was alone, and she was curled up in the limb of an old tree staring straight ahead, not really seeing Tanya as she approached her.

"Angel?"

Tanya touched her arm, but Angel felt like stone and didn't move. Tanya stood back not knowing what to do. Should she just leave Angel alone? Obviously Angel did not come to the manor to be consoled by May, she came to be alone.

"Angel, look at me."

Angel didn't respond, and Tanya continued, "Did you see May and does she know what's happened?"

No reply.

Tanya decided to leave her and find May. She headed for the front door of the manor but decided first to go to Angel's car and see if the keys were there. She snatched the keys from the car and went back to the manor.

All was quiet as she stepped inside, and Tanya assumed that Angel never came in. She also wondered why May never heard the car.

"May," she called. But when there was no reply, she tiptoed through the house and peek into the partially open doorway leading to May's bedroom. The room was in semi darkness and she heard May snoring.

She knew for a fact now that Angel never came into the house to tell her aunt. She wondered what she should do next. She couldn't leave Rachael and Mae for long. What if her little niece all of sudden realized what had happened and Rachael couldn't control her sorrow? Tanya felt the burden on her shoulders. She had to get help, but where?

Angel's aunt drew a long breath and woke herself from a snore. Her eyes were bright and wide as she noticed Tanya. "What's going on? Why are you staring at me?"

Tanya realized that Angel's aunt had lived a long life, and had seen lots of sorrow throughout. She counted on her to now help console Angel and the girls.

"May, I've got some bad news."

May sat up in the bed and continued to stare at Tanya.

"It's Jake, May. He was in a car accident, and…he didn't make it."

May's shoulders drooped. She sat calmly, her eyes blinking as if thinking. "Where's Angel and the girls?"

Tanya knew she'd found the help she needed.

****

Rachael couldn't concentrate on making small talk to Mae. Mae seemed in another world, one they all enjoyed living in yesterday. It hadn't sunk into Mae's brain that her dad had just died.

Rachael didn't even want to be in Mae's room. She wanted to be in her cubby hole alone so she could cry her eyes out. The lump in her throat hurt and was getting bigger, as she tried to swallow the tears that kept forming behind her eyeballs. But she knew she had to keep up the façade until someone came back to the house to rescue her and to take over being with Mae.

The minutes dragged into almost an hour. Mae asked Rachael where their mother was, and wasn't it time for Daddy to be home? Rachael saw it as a chance to once again explain to her sister what had happened.

"Mae, Daddy is not coming home tonight. He was in a terrible car accident today on his way home and he got terribly hurt and he died."

It had been so hard to say the words, *he died*, but this time it sank in and Mae started to cry, as if it were the first time she had heard the news.

Rachael put her arms out and Mae ran to her. "Mae, I know this is hard, but you must try and be brave for Mom. I…I don't even know where she is." Rachael's own tears began.

"Is that why Mommy was screaming?"

"Yes, Mae."

The two girls wept together and Rachael at least felt relieved that now she did not have to pretend anymore.

****

Tanya so admired the strength shining in the old woman's eyes. She was being strong, hiding her own grief and thinking of her niece and her children.

"Angel's outside in the orchard, staring off into space. If you think you feel up to it, I'd like you to come back to the house with me and stay with the girls."

"Of course," May replied. "I'll just get my things together, but I want to see Angel first."

"Okay, May, you know best. She might open up to you and break through her wall of silence."

May gathered up her things, ready to be with the girls for as long as it took. Tanya took May's things to the car then returned to the manor to help May walk to the orchard.

May refused any help and leaned on her cane, mumbling, "Hate this thing, but I've had an old flare up in my leg, the one that was broken you know, when I fell off the ladder trying to paint the top of the window frame."

When May saw Angel sitting in the crook of the big tree branch, she forged ahead forgetting about her leg. She reached Angel's side and demanded, "Get up, child and lean on your auntie now."

As if she were hypnotized, Angel rose from the tree branch and walked with arms outstretched into her aunt's waiting arms.

"Oh, May, why did this happen? What am I going to do now?" Angel bawled and there seemed to be no end to it.

Thinking that May might be getting tired, Tanya approached the older woman and managed to get Angel to lean on her. "Angel, you have to leave the orchard now and come home. Rachael and Mae need you."

Angel put an arm around Tanya and walked like a zombie, followed by May, until they had left the orchard. The three women got into Tanya's car and drove to Angel's house.

****

Rachael heard a car door slam and jumped up, leaving Mae still sitting on the bed. She hurried to the window and looked down. She saw her Aunt Tanya get out of her car and walk around to the passenger side and open the door.

Aunt May got out of the back door. She leaned heavily on her cane and carefully managed to get herself out of the car. She shut the back door and waited until Tanya helped Angel out of the front seat.

"Is that Mommy?" Mae wanted to know.

"Yes. And Aunt Tanya and Aunt May." Rachael turned back to the window. She watched Angel turn to Aunt May and lean heavily on her. Rachael saw her Aunt Tanya carefully replace Aunt May with herself, helping Angel up the walk and onto the front veranda.

"Mae, stay in your room for a bit. I'm going down to see what's going on, okay?" Mae didn't respond and she seemed to Rachael to have gone once more into shock.

Rachael went into the hall and watched the women move towards the stairs. Rachael stayed put as the trio passed her and headed for her mother and father's bedroom. Rachael heard a click as the bedroom door closed. She waited, wondering what would happen next.

CHAPTER TWO

Tanya and May helped Angel settle on her bed. Angel was reluctant at first, but May said, "Lie down, child. It's the best thing for you to do now."

Tanya was relieved that Angel listened to May and followed directions. She knew a sedative was in order, but wasn't sure there were any in the house. Comfortable that Angel's aunt had everything under control momentarily, Tanya left the bedroom and headed out to see Rachael and Mae.

Rachael looked up as her Aunt Tanya entered Mae's bedroom. She was full of questions but she didn't know how to begin asking them.

Mae looked up and said in a calm voice, "Hi, Aunt Tanya."

Tanya went immediately and hugged the little girl. Next she went to Rachael. Rachael's only question was, "Can I leave now?" Tanya nodded and Rachael made her departure, straight to her cubby hole.

Tanya left Mae in her room and went to the bathroom. She opened the cabinet and rooted around, finding a bottle with Angel's name on it. One before bedtime for sleep. They would have to do for now. If Angel could sleep it would be the best thing for her and for everyone else right now as well. Tanya padded into Angel's bedroom with a glass of water and a tablet in her hand.

May sat by Angel's bed still trying to convince her that it was best that she stay lying down for a while. She spied the glass of water and realized that Tanya had something in her hand.

"Angel, sit up, dear," May encouraged. "Tanya has something for you that will help."

Angel sat up and looked curiously at Tanya. "What is it?"

"Just a sleeping pill from your cabinet."

"I haven't taken any of those for months. They knock me out."

"Then take one now," May ordered.

****

Outside in her cubby hole, Rachael was not as contented there as she thought she would be. While looking after Mae she longed to get away by herself. Now, all the silence and aloneness did was make her think of her father. Flashes of his face, smiling, laughing, were before her.

Suddenly she was a little girl again, running behind her father and asking, "Where are we going, Daddy? Daddy, you walk too fast."

"Catch up, Star, it's a surprise."

Star had been a nickname that Angel had given her when they first met. Rachael had only been four years old but she remembered meeting Angel…the pretty lady that lived at the manor. She didn't remember why Angel and her Dad called her Star and one day her new mother told her.

"We were upstairs in the manor and you asked me if my real name was Angel and if I was really an angel. I assured you I was not but that my real name was Angelique, and my nickname was Angel. You wanted a nickname so you became Star because you liked stars and said you're daddy had told you that your mom was now a star in heaven."

Rachael's thoughts returned to her father and the day he'd brought her to her new tree house. They climbed the ladder to the top and Rachael had peeked inside. "It's kinda dark in there, Daddy, why doesn't it have a window?"

"It does, Rachael. See that knob? Slide it."

Rachael pushed the knob over and opened the little wooden window. A ray of bright sunlight entered the tree house.

"When you want light you can open it, and when you want to be alone with your thoughts, you can close it."

"Neat." Rachael laughed. "Oh, Daddy, it's beautiful and just what I've always wanted. It's my…my little cubby hole."

Jake laughed. "Well, Star, we all need a place to think sometimes. This is yours."

"Just for me? And no one else can come inside?"

"Only if you invite them."

Rachael jammed her fists in her eyes trying to send the images and memories away. It was just too painful to think about him right now. It was all tumbling in on her. The truth was surfacing like a giant wave from a tsunami. The painful grief washed over her and felt like someone was beating her to the ground. She cried until she could barely breathe.

****

Now that Angel had finally fallen asleep, May left the bedroom and went to look in on her niece. As she entered the bedroom door, Mae was sitting at her desk drawing. So like her mother this child, and yet so like her father in many ways. Mae had the fortitude and strength of her father, and the sensitive side of her mother. She was quite a combination.

"That's a really pretty picture," May said, while looking over young Mae's shoulder.

Mae looked up at her great aunt's wrinkled face. "It's the orchard, where Mommy and Daddy like to walk. Why are you here, Aunt May? I didn't know you were visiting."

"I'm here to watch over you."

Mae continued drawing, placing a few apples on one of the trees. She suddenly remarked, "Is it because of Daddy?"

"Well, I'm here to keep you company, is that okay?"

"Sure."

"Are you hungry? I hear Tanya in the kitchen. I think she's making something."

Mae nodded but kept drawing.

"Well, let's go to the kitchen and see what she has."

Mae followed her great aunt down the stairs, but when it took her aunt too long to get down, Mae forged ahead of her and waited for her at the bottom.

May stopped in the hallway and listened. All was quiet in the upstairs of Angel and Jake's home.

****

Rachael stopped crying, as if she had become cried out. She sat in the quiet of her cubby hole with the little wooden door closed tightly. She listened to the breeze outside her containment and wondered how things could change so quickly. How could their night that they all had looked forward to have changed so horribly?

Her dad should be home by now and they should be out at the *Captain's Cave* enjoying a meal together, because her dad had made the reservation two days earlier. He wanted to make sure they got a good table by the window so they could watch the boats in the harbour.

Rachael remembered the days on the sailing boat. First it had just been her mom and dad and herself. Then after Mae had come along there were the four of them. Always an adventure, and sometimes they would stay on the boat, sleep on it, and go far enough out so they could fish.

Rachael remembered Mae's first fish and how she helped her little sister reel it in. Such wonderful memories all dashed to nothing now. There would be no dinner at the *Captain's Cave*. Her dad would not be home. She would not see him again. She would never hear his wonderful laugh or play ball with him in the backyard. He would not take them for winter rides again on his snowmobile, up the long and winding woods' road behind their house.

Rachael wiped the tears from her eyes and wondered what was happening in the house. She wanted to know. She wanted to be around her family now, she had had enough alone time.

****

William Canton sat on a hospital bed wishing he could get out of there. The conversation with Jake's daughter had been disturbing. He hadn't wanted to tell her what he had to, but he had to.

Poor Jake. Bill was feeling responsible. If he hadn't had his car in the shop, maybe Jake wouldn't have been on the road on his way home from Halifax. He would have been home right now with Angel and the girls.

Damn. It was such poor timing and now his friend was gone. He couldn't imagine what was going on in the Jordan household at that minute. The girl had sounded hysterical, which of course she was entitled to be. When he had called Angel, he was still in shock himself. If he hadn't been he would have thought better of it. Better to leave that up to the RCMP to do. But it was too late now. Should he have told the girl what she wanted to know? It would always be something he was not sure of the answer, but she insisted and he felt he had to.

"Mr. Canton?" Bill was relieved to see a nurse come in. "You're free to go now. Just see your doctor in a couple of days to see how that head wound is coming along."

Bill nodded. There was no need for words. Besides he wasn't in the mood for talking. The crash returned to his memory every so often, but he blinked, swallowed and shoved it away. He didn't want to think about it today. Hell, he didn't want to ever think about it again, but he knew that was impossible. Damn, why did that guy have to come over the middle line? Was he drunk? Heart attack or some other kind of seizure? Why then? Why ever?

Bill collected his stuff as best he could. His arm was in a sling, just a sprain they had said. His leg hurt, just torn ligaments, they told him. The gash on his head hurt, his head ached savagely, but he was walking and he could be talking if he wanted to.

He left the hospital room wondering how he would get home from the city. Maybe he would call his brother, Eric. After all Eric owed him.

****

Jake is smiling at her. He's standing in the orchard in front of the old barn. He appears to be pruning the branches on an old apple tree. Angel finds it strange that Jake is doing this. He had never shown an interest in anything like that before. She walks towards him but feels more like she is floating.

"What are you doing?" she asks.

"Making your orchard look beautiful," he replies. "Because you love it so."

Angel reaches for him but Jake becomes see-through and disappears. Angel screams and wakes up.

Covered in sweat and shaking, she threw back the heavy cover that had been over her. "Jake," she screamed. "Where are you?"

The door flew open and Tanya, Rachael, and Aunt May stood in the doorway, each one trying to get through it first.

Aunt May made it through. "It's okay, Angel," she soothed.

Angel trembled. She was back to reality and wishing she was still in the lovely dream. "It's not okay, Aunt May. It will never be okay again. Jake is gone. My love, my life." Angel broke into tears and even Aunt May couldn't comfort her.

Rachael moved closer. She didn't want to push Aunt May out of the way, but she wanted desperately to be near her mother. She slid around Aunt May and fell into Angel's arms.

"Mom. What are we going to do?"

Angel comforted Rachael. Calm now, she knew she must be strong. She had two daughters who were hurting as much as she was. All at once she thought of Mae and inquired, "Where's your sister? I want to see her. Tanya, can you get Mae?"

Angel hugged Rachael to her breast. She touched her hair and kissed the top of her head. "We're going to get through this, Star, somehow. You know before I woke up I was dreaming of your father. We were in the orchard and he was pruning an apple tree."

Rachael pulled back from Angel's embrace and looked at her mother. "Why was he doing that? Dad never did that sort of thing. He didn't know anything about apple trees except he liked to eat the apples."

"I know. It was so strange. But he said he did it for me, because I loved the orchard so much."

Mae entered the bedroom, looking shy and standoffish. Angel opened her arms to her youngest daughter, the daughter that she and Jake had created. "Come here, baby, come be with Rachael and me."

The three of them embraced on the bed and cried openly. Mae asked her mother why, and Angel was unable to give her daughter an answer. Tanya and Aunt May looked on.

"Some alone time will be helpful," May whispered to Tanya and they both left the bedroom.

****

William Canton walked out the big hospital doors to be greeted by his brother, Eric. Eric was taller than Bill. He was gangly but young enough to make up for it in the future years when many men started putting on weight.

"Hey, bro." Eric tried to sound upbeat.

"Hey, yourself," Bill replied.

The brothers hugged and continued on down to the parking lot where Eric took the driver's seat. Bill pulled the passenger door shut and pushed off the radio button. It had been blaring out some rock tune or other.

"Hey, don't like my music?"

"I'm not in the mood, okay?"

Eric got serious. "Yeah, I know. You were damn lucky. But that poor guy, Jake, he didn't see it coming, eh?"

Bill wished he didn't have to talk. But it was an hour's drive and sooner or later he would have to anyway. He sighed and touched his head, lightly caressing the bandage that was plastered across his forehead.

"No, he didn't see it coming, and I didn't see it coming either. It…just happened. And for the life of me, I can't stop feeling guilty about it."

"Guilty? Why?"

"Because Jake probably wouldn't have been on the highway today, if it hadn't been for me."

"Why were you driving together anyway?"

"My car's in the shop. I had an important meeting and I had just run into Jake at the coffee shop downtown. I was going in and he was coming out. I asked him if he knew anyone going into the city, told him I had an appointment at ten and so far I wasn't having any luck. I tried to rent a car, but I was having trouble organizing that. In fact, I had just come out of a car rental place and all their vehicles were rented. I decided to pick up a coffee and phone another place to see if I had better luck there.

"Jake said, no problem. He had some stuff he could do in the city and his day wasn't busy in the Valley so he'd take me. He said, get your coffee and hop in. I was relieved to say the least. It was an important meeting. I was finally selling off the house and had to be at the bank to sign papers."

"You could've cancelled."

Bill gave his brother the eye. "Yeah, I could've done a lot of things differently, like not taking my car to the shop. It was working, just not right. And if I had seen things ahead, I would have not taken it in."

"Well, you can't change the past."

"Look, Eric. I know you're trying to be cooperative, but this isn't getting me anywhere. It doesn't make me feel any better and in fact, it's making me feel worse. So shut up, will you?"

But Eric wouldn't quit. "I just don't see though why you feel guilty. You didn't create the accident. You were just a passenger—"

"I know. But, hell, if Jake hadn't been driving me today, he wouldn't have been in that particular spot on the highway, don't you get it? And besides, the car hit the driver's side, not the passenger side where I was."

"Well," Eric continued, "you can look at it another way. It might have been you driving home at that particular time on that particular spot, and I wouldn't be sitting here driving you home now, or even talking to you, bro."

"Goddamnit, kid, you have a weird way of looking at things. And you know what? I wish I had been driving and it had been me. Jake Jordan had the world by the tail, successful in business, happy home life, not the miserable mess I've made out of my life. What am I? Retired early, actually kicked out of my company. Divorced from a woman who couldn't keep her panties on. Living alone, without any kids to my name. Yep, Jake Jordan didn't deserve to die today."

"And you did?"

"More than he did."

"Ah, come on."

"Come on yourself. Even you have a better future ahead of you than I do."

"Oh, great, thanks. Your faith in me is soooo appreciated."

"Look, if I had another way to get home, today, I wouldn't have called you."

"You mean you wouldn't have bothered me, right?"

"Right."

"Big brother, always the independent one. Never needed anything from anyone, right?"

"I said, shut up, Eric."

"No, you listen. It's not my fault that our mother favours me. It's not my fault that I happened to be brainy enough to get scholarships, so she didn't have to go around telling everyone that she had to sacrifice like hell to put me through university like she did with you. And it's not my fault that she compares you to our dad in every way, and not in a good way."

"I know it's not your fault. So…enough."

Eric finally stopped talking and the rest of the journey home was silent. He pulled into Bill's yard and kept the motor running. Bill got out.

"Thanks for the lift. Now I owe you."

Eric grinned. "No problem, bro. Take it easy, eh? And for fuck's sake, stop feeling guilty over this."

CHAPTER THREE

The following few days in the Jordan household were sombre and sometimes filled with hysterical crying. There were a few good moments, and some really bad ones.

Tanya volunteered to be at the house with Angel and the girls as much as she could during the day. She took care of the phone calls and the funeral arrangements with Rachael and May's help, and she did what she could to see that everyone was fed and the house was tidied up.

She wished that her dad was here, but he and her mother were in Europe, and although they had planned to return, it would not be until the day before the funeral.

Angel had seen her doctor and was now taking a sedative to help her cope. This pretty much left her either sleeping most of the time, or staring into space.

Rachael helped Tanya at times, and even little Mae helped out. Angel's Aunt May went back to the manor. She told Tanya that she knew the girls and Angel were in good hands.

Tanya didn't feel as staunch as a brick but that had been the way May had described her. She had been grateful though to her wonderful husband who told her to be with the girls, they needed her. She knew how much Bob needed her too. He was not a well man. Strong and sturdy for the first thirty-five years of his life, but then it happened. Multiple Sclerosis. Two years ago he had been diagnosed and since then he was becoming progressively worse. Tanya had her hands full, but she was where Bob wanted her to be. He was still able to look after himself in some ways. So she scooted back and forth from her house to Angel's.

****

The morning was sunny, it should have been rain. Angel woke to the feel of sun on her face. It streamed in the patio doors, and although she wanted to stay in bed forever, she knew she had to get up and go through the motions of living.

The thought of Jake's funeral was too much to think of. She rolled out of bed and tossed her housecoat around her shoulders. Trying to keep from falling apart, she walked to the patio doors and opened them.

The sun fell on her face. She closed her eyes, remembering the day so long ago, it seemed, that she and Jake and little Rachael had stood there, in this very month of August, and declared to everyone that had come to May's seventy-fifth birthday party, that they were getting married.

The crowd below had applauded in grand style and then they, the three of them, a family to be, had walked down the stairs together and joined the party. Rachael had been in her swimsuit after her tumble in the pool. All the big misunderstanding between Jake and Angel had been resolved and the day had been beautiful.

Angel's Aunt May had cornered her to further talk about the sale of the manor. "Aunt May, if only you had told me what was taking place, none of this misunderstanding today would have happened."

May had looked at her scornfully. "I don't know how you could have even considered that Jake was selling me out. Jake would never do a thing like that."

"I know better now, Aunt May, but I don't know Jake yet, like you do."

"You will in time, child. You will in time."

And it was true. She had come to know Jake as if he were part of her. The marriage might have been only fifteen years, but it was a lifetime that would never be replaced. No one could ever take the place of Jake in her life. Why, her life was nothing without Jake. From now on she vowed to live for her daughters, although she was only in her forties.

A knock brought Angel back to the present and she turned to see Tanya standing in the doorway. "Good morning, Angel. Breakfast is ready."

Angel walked to the doorway and put her arms around Tanya. She laid her head on her sister-in-law's shoulder. "Thank you for being here. What would we do without you?"

Tanya patted Angel's shoulder. "You'll do okay. It just takes time."

Angel pulled back and looked into Tanya's eyes. "How do you do it, Tanya? How do you come here day after day and stay so strong?"

Tanya smiled. "I don't know. I just keep going. I've gotten this way with Bob I guess, and it's the only way I can survive."

Angel put her arm across Tanya's shoulder and they went downstairs to breakfast.

****

The cemetery where Jake was to be laid to rest was on a hill overlooking a beautiful pond. Ducks quacked and fluttered their wings as the gathering stood on a mound and said their farewell to a man they had known, as father, son, husband, friend, brother, and business associate.

Angel wept silently when the casket was placed in the ground. She promised herself that on this day of days she would keep it all together, for her daughters at least. Mae stood by her side holding her hand. She was quiet and didn't cry. Jake's parents, Raymond and Marjorie, were next to Mae. Rachael was holding onto her Aunt Tanya, weeping openly. Tanya's husband, Bob sat in his wheelchair next to Tanya. Angel's Aunt May stood silently at the end, like the trooper that she was.

When the ceremony was over, many people came forward to offer condolences to Angel and her family. Angel knew most of them, but there was one man, standing on the outskirts of the group, that she didn't know. He walked with a limp and his arm was in a sling. There was a bandage on his forehead, and Angel wondered who he was.

"Do you know him?" Angel asked Tanya, while pointing to the stranger.

Tanya gazed in the direction and replied, "No, never saw him before."

"I wonder why he's here," Angel muttered.

Rachael, who stood beside her asked, "Do you want me to find out?"

"No, it's okay. Just curious I guess."

But Rachael wasn't satisfied and thought it might be the man she talked to on the phone. Leaving the gathering she wandered over in the man's direction. He seemed to be standing alone, so she approached him.

"Excuse me," she said.

The man turned to face her.

"Do we know you?"

"Not really," the man said. "But I knew your father."

"And you look kinda messed up. Are you the man I talked to on the phone?"

"If you're Rachael, yes I am."

"Are you hurt badly?"

"No. Nothing serious. A sprained wrist, cut on the head."

"Lucky."

"Yes…I guess. Look, I'm sorry—"

"It's okay. Nothing you can do now. Excuse me."

Rachael went back to the gathering and saw Angel engaged in a conversation with May's old friend, Arnold Brooks.

She waited for them to stop talking then approached Angel. "He's the man that was riding with Dad."

"What?"

"I said—"

"I know what you said, and I've got to talk to him."

"Mom." Rachael stopped. It was no use, once her mom got something in her head, no one could stop her. Rachael turned and looked for Mae. It was time to go.

Angel hurried across the grass and walked up to the man, who had his back to her. He turned when he heard her call, "You there, I want to see you." Angel stopped in front of the man as he turned. "Who are you?" she asked.

"I'm William Canton, a friend of your husband."

"Rachael tells me you're the one who called from the hospital."

"Yes, I did."

"How could you?"

"Ah…I don't know what you mean?"

"That was a terrible thing to do. A phone call out of the blue telling me that my husband was dead. Do you have any idea what that was like?"

"Ma'am, I'm sorry. I shouldn't have, but I hardly knew what I was doing myself. I called before I thought. My apologies to you. It would have been better had—"

"It was wrong, just wrong. But I guess I had to find out somehow. What happened?"

"Ma'am, I hardly think this is the right place for that."

"Well, I need to know all the details. I want to know what Jake was saying and where you were when it happened. Why was my Jake even there?" Angel couldn't help it, the tears streamed out of her eyes. "Why did he die? What made the accident happen?"

"Mrs Jordan, I'm more than willing to tell you what I can, but this is not the place or the day. I'm sorry. I'm even sorry that I came today. I didn't mean to upset you."

"Fine, then. You obviously have my phone number so you call me when you can talk about it, and we'll get together somewhere and discuss this. We will get to the bottom of this." Angel turned and ran back to the top of the hill, where Tanya and the others were waiting.

****

"Where's your mother?" Tanya asked.

"As soon as we got home, she went to her bedroom. I gave her a sedative and I think she's gone to sleep," Rachael replied.

How could such a beautiful sunny day hold such emptiness? Rachael went upstairs to look for Mae. Feeling like she not only had to be a big sister to Mae but also a mom now.

"Hey, Mae, whatcha doing?"

Mae looked up from her desk. "Drawing."

"Oh. Can I see?"

"Sure you can see. It's a fantasy castle. See. Look at the alligators swimming in the moat." Mae smiled. "Do you like it?"

"Ah…sure, I guess." Rachael tried hard to understand her little sister. At the funeral she never once saw her cry. Now she was acting like they had just come back from ice cream.

"Mae, do you understand what happened to Dad?"

Mae nodded.

"Are you sad about it?"

Mae nodded again.

"Then how come you never cried today? Don't you miss him?"

Tears swelled in Mae's eyes and she abandoned her drawing. Her arms went around her big sister's waist and she sobbed on her stomach. "I do. I miss him so much. But Mommy is so sad. I don't want to upset her."

Rachael got down on her knees next to her sister. "Oh, Mae. You don't have to be strong for Mom, that's her job. You don't have to hold in the tears, at least not when you're with me."

Mae clung to her big sister and let the tears flow freely. They wept together in the privacy of Mae's room.

****

Tanya faced a heavy burden. With the funeral over, she knew that it was now up to her to look after Angel and Jake's affairs. She wished that Angel would be more helpful but realized that the shock of Jake's death had wounded her greatly, to the point of almost non-existence. Tanya had taken on the responsibility, for the time being anyway, of dealing with Jake's lawyer and executor of his estate. She believed that things were in order, but they would need Angel's input for future decisions. However, Angel seemed unable to participate.

The following week after the funeral, Tanya noticed an improvement in Angel. She interacted more with the children and took over the kitchen duties. It seemed to be the change that Tanya was looking for, so she approached Angel when she was putting dishes in the dishwasher.

"You seem to be feeling better, Angel."

Angel closed the dishwasher door and turned to her. "I'm doing what I have to. Life goes on it seems. And you, Tanya need to get back to your home and your husband. You won't need to come over everyday anymore."

"Well, I do want to help you with the business stuff. I think everything seems in order but perhaps we should all meet up, the executor and Jake's lawyer—"

"I agree," Angel said. "And I would appreciate you being with me. Rachael has also been such a great help to me lately. One would almost think she was Mae's mother rather than I." She smiled, and it was the first smile Tanya had seen on Angel's face since Jake's death. "Of course that will end soon enough when Rachael has to go back to college."

"Yes, and that's going to be very hard on her, I believe."

"Well, don't you think anymore about it, you have enough on your hands as it is."

Tanya was relieved to hear those words coming from Angel. Finally she would be able to spend some quality time with Bob. "If you think you're up to it, Angel. I do need to get back to Bob. He's been so very patient with all of this. And he needs me more than he'll let on."

Angel was glad that Tanya wanted to return to her home and her own duties. She felt like an intruder in her own home for a while now. In her heart she realized that she had to get back to the land of the living. Jake was not coming home. Jake was not going to make decisions for the family any longer. It was now up to her, and she felt the weight of it like an albatross around her shoulders.

****

Angel knew what day it was, but she hadn't talked about it, and neither did her daughters. It was time. She called both Rachael and Mae into the kitchen.

"Mae," she said. "I know it's your birthday, and normally we'd all make a big deal out of it, you know that. But…" She looked at both her daughters who were sitting at the counter but not interrupting. "But, this year, things are a little different. However, I do want to celebrate your birthday, and I want it to be a happy event. So let's say we put all other thoughts out of our head today and have a nice supper with your aunts, May and Tanya, and your uncle, Bob."

Rachael was the first up. She strolled over to the cupboards and opened one of the cabinet doors. Reaching in, she said, "And, I've got the cake already."

Mae's eyes lit up as Rachael produced a fluffy pink cake with blue candles on it and an elephant as a centrepiece.

"Rachael," Angel declared, "you were sneaking around behind my back, how good of you." Angel laughed, and it was the first true laugh that she'd heard come from her own mouth in ages.

The girls got excited and Rachael said she'd call her aunts and see if they were available to come over for supper. Angel busied herself with asking Mae what she would like for supper.

"I want Daddy's favourite, spaghetti and meatballs. And I want oatmeal cookies on the side."

Angel remembered how much Jake had loved oatmeal cookies and how she learned to make them just right from Aunt May's recipe. "And so it will be, Mae. It's your birthday after all." The mention of Jake and the request of his favourite meal did not upset Angel. She thought it was a great way to include Jake in his daughter's birthday celebration.

Tanya was unable to attend, saying that she and Bob had made other plans earlier. But Angel went over to the manor and brought May to the party. When she got there Arnold was visiting. Ever since Arnold's wife Mabel had passed away the year before, he had been spending a lot of time visiting with May and playing cards. So Arnold came along for the birthday celebration as well.

It was an evening of joyous celebration, and Angel presented Mae with her very own easel and set of oil paints that her dad had bought for her earlier in the month. Angel's heart swelled when Mae said she would try and paint a portrait of her father someday. Angel just knew that somewhere Jake was proudly approving of this birthday celebration.

\

CHAPTER FOUR

Meeting with Angel Jordan was something that William Canton was not looking forward to. He regretted going to Jake's funeral at all, but he had wanted to pay his respects to a fine man and a friend. Although they had not been close friends, Jake and he had been business friends for a couple of years.

Bill had moved to the Valley after the messy divorce with his wife, Lorraine. He didn't want to live in the house they had built together, and he no longer wanted to be around their friends on a daily basis.

Lorraine had drained him financially. Although there had been no children in their marriage, she had become involved with a lawyer friend of his and needless to say, Bill came out on the losing end of everything. He cringed when he thought of Andrew Bachman. The thought of even calling him a friend these days made him sick to his stomach. A friend did not covet another friend's wife. A friend did not go for the jugular in divorce proceedings either. In the end, his wife and he had split the value of the house and put it on the market. Unfortunately it took two years to sell, and ended up being rented during that time.

Now, finally free of the house, Bill had acquired some extra money that he could put to good use. He had contented himself with living on a lake. He loved to fish and found solitude was good for the soul. Now he wondered how he would deal with Jake's widow. She was not about to forgive easily, even though he felt in his heart that she did not rightfully blame him for Jake's death, she did insinuate that he was part of the cause. He agreed, and he dealt with the guilt every day since the accident.

****

Angel's first meeting with William Canton happened four days after Mae's birthday. He had called her and asked her if she still wanted to talk. Angel had been thinking about their earlier meeting at the cemetery and wondered if he would ever call her about it. When he did, she was ready for him and asked him to meet her at a park across from the Tourist Bureau.

Angel was there first. She sat and watched the water gurgling down a little stream that wound its way through the park. It was peaceful there and private. A dark blue Toyota Yaris pulled into the parking lot. Angel turned to see a medium height man in blue jeans and white T-shirt get out. He had a military style haircut, blue eyes that were quite ordinary looking, and thick brows. He had an angled jaw, with a light beard and lips that were thin but well shaped. She recognized him as William Canton. He wore a pained expression on his deeply tanned face as he walked towards her. Angel decided to be pleasant.

"Hello," she called to him.

He acknowledged her greeting with a smile. "Hello, Mrs Jordan. Nice spot here."

"And quite private," she replied.

Angel got up from the bench she had been sitting on and asked, "Would you like to walk?"

"Not really. My leg isn't up to it yet."

"Oh, of course. I'm sorry. I see you've lost your sling."

"Yes. It was just a wrist strain." He felt he sounded like he was making light of his injuries after what had happened to Jake. But if truth be told, he didn't know what to say to this woman.

"So, let's get right to the point," Angel said. "Why were you driving with Jake?"

"Jake offered to drive me to the city because my car was in for repair."

"Okay, he picked you up and you were driving home. Right outside of Windsor on the two-way road, you and Jake were driving along, probably not going too fast, were you?"

"I imagine we were going the speed limit. Jake was not a fast driver."

"That's true. So, exactly what was going on in the car?"

"Mrs Jordan, I really don't remember—"

"Well, think."

Angel raised her voice and he could see she was getting agitated. He tried to recall the day. He took a long breath. "I believe he was telling me about Mae's birthday coming up and how he'd bought her paints or something."

Angel smiled. "Yes he did. He bought her a set of oil paints. What else?"

He sighed. "Something about you painting. And how you had painted a portrait of his other daughter, Rachael when she was small. He said it hung in the living room." Angel smiled again. It seemed to be doing her good to hear this so he tried harder to remember what he could. "I think just before it happened he was telling me what a fine artist you were and how you…and then we saw the car. It was so quick, neither of us had time to say anything. I closed my eyes and felt the impact and heard the crash. It was like slow motion. When I opened them I looked over at Jake…and you don't want to hear this."

"Yes, I do. I want to hear it all."

"All I can tell you is that I believe he died instantly. I passed out then so I don't recall anything else, until I was being rescued from the car by the paramedics. There's no more to tell you."

Angel slumped on the bench and covered her face with her hands. She closed her eyes and pictured what she had just heard. If he was right, and this was what she had been told by the RCMP also, then Jake did die instantly. She was glad of that at least. She could not think of her darling lying in pain. She rose and looked away from Bill. "Thank you, Mr. Canton, for telling me Jake's last thoughts. In a way it's comforting."

Although she'd wanted details from the man that Jake had spent his last hours with, she was not prepared for the flood of feelings that she felt for him, and they were not good feelings. In a way, she resented him, was jealous of him for being with Jake at the end when she wasn't. She turned to him and knew that her face did not show kindness. "But I can't help it, Mr. Canton, I still feel that you're partly to blame for Jake's death, and he died and you didn't."

He wished he'd never come. She was overwrought with misery, and he couldn't blame her for wanting to pin the blame on him. But he couldn't take anymore. He wrestled daily with the guilt himself, and he didn't need this from her. "I'm sorry, Mrs Jordan. I do understand how you would feel that way. I'd...better go."

"I'm sorry, but this is how I feel. I apologize for my feelings but they are what they are." She watched him get up and limp back to his car. Was she wrong to say what she did? She knew she had hurt him, but in a way it had made her feel better. In her heart she knew that this was not William Canton's fault, but she couldn't get past it, not yet anyway.

****

Since her meeting with the man in Jake's car, Angel developed a strange sort of relationship with him in her mind. The meeting had been very emotional, and Angel felt that he was her only tie to Jake. She was not through with William Canton yet, but in her heart she knew deep down that she would probably never be satisfied with any explanations of that horrible day.

Mae had returned to school and Rachael was getting ready to leave for college and her second year of pre-vet studies. Angel knew how much she'd miss her and how hard it was going to be for Rachael to concentrate after all that had happened. She also knew that Rachael was reluctant to go but was going through the motions of preparing for it anyway.

It had been three weeks now since Jake had died and it seemed as if all of their lives before the accident had been lived by someone else. Angel went upstairs to see how Rachael was making out with her packing.

She stood in her daughter's doorway remembering the day she'd first met her. Rachael had been only four years old and what a beauty she had been She was still a beautiful girl, a young woman now. Rachael was digging through her closet, and when she heard Angel approach, she stuck her head out and grinned at her. Angel noticed the same sweet set of dimples in her cheeks that she had noticed the first day she'd met Rachael. And she remembered seeing pictures of Jake's first wife and realizing how startling the resemblance was between her and Rachael. Now that Rachael was grown, she had become even more like her mother in looks, same blonde hair, same dimples, same smile.

"So much to do, I don't know where to start, Mom." Rachael looked defeated and Angel went to her, putting her arms around her daughter.

"Let's start with a big hug then we'll get down to the nitty-gritty."

Rachael laughed and pulled out her luggage from the closet floor. Just as she was zipping the biggest case open, the phone on her desk rang. Rachael grabbed it and said hello. She listened for a bit then replied, "Arnold, calm down. I can't understand a thing you're saying. Here's Mom." Rachael passed the phone to her mother and said, "It's Arnold, he's yelling in the phone and I can't make him out."

Angel took the phone and spoke in a calm voice, "What is it Arnold, where are you? What's that about May? What? I'll be right there."

Angel slammed down the phone. "Arnold's over at May's and he said she fell. And he said, she passed out, and she won't wake up. Call 911. I'm going over."

Rachael grabbed the phone, and Angel ran down the stairs and jumped in her car. It wasn't that far to the manor, she would be there in less than five minutes."

****

When Angel arrived, the paramedics still had not. She dashed from her car and up the manor steps onto the porch. Arnold Brooks flew through the screen door, shaking his head and waving his red hanky with the white dots.

"She's on the floor, Angel," he yelled.

Angel hurried into the hallway and turned towards the living room. There she saw her darling Aunt May lying stretched out on the floor. Angel bent over her and tapped her cheeks and shook her shoulders lightly. "May, can you hear me? May, open your eyes."

Angel was still hovering over her aunt when the paramedics rushed into the living room. Angel rose and stepped back, relieved to see the team go to work. She was staring at the scene when Arnold returned from outside.

"We were just talkin', Angel. May told me she was feelin' dizzy then before I could reply, she sank to the floor. I tried to rouse her but she didn't respond, that's when I called you."

Long lanky Arnold had terror in his eyes. He was ninety-one and shouldn't be getting so upset, Angel thought. "You did the right thing, Arnold," she said, putting an arm across his shoulder and leading him to the sofa to sit down.

Arnold stared at the proceedings going on around May, and Angel couldn't tear her eyes away either. Then there was a stop in the previous action and one of the paramedics got up and walked towards the duo on the sofa.

"I'm afraid we're too late. The lady is gone."

Angel's hands flew to her mouth. She couldn't believe what she'd heard. In fact Angel felt herself slipping from the sofa and blackness surrounded her.

Arnold jumped up and stood horrified staring at the collapsed Angel lying at his feet. The paramedic that had been speaking to Angel bent down and took her blood pressure. Another paramedic, noticing Arnold, got up and walked towards him. She put a hand on his shoulder and led him outside. She guided him to the porch swing and also took his blood pressure.

"What's goin' on in there?" Arnold wanted to know. "I don't want to be out here. I'm all right. I want to be with my friend. That's May in there you know, and her niece, Angel. Why are you keepin' me out here?"

The paramedic tried to calm him, as the gurney rolled out the manor door. Angel was walking behind. Arnold began to weep and pulled the hanky from his jeans pocket to mop his eyes.

****

It was just three weeks since the family had been to the cemetery and laid Jake to rest. Today they had returned to say goodbye to May Driscoll, beloved aunt, sister and friend to many.

Angel watched Arnold take a shovel of dirt and throw it on top of May's casket. Angel knew he always loved her in his way, although he'd been married to Mabel for all of his life, until she had passed on. Over the past year, since Mabel's death, he had spent a lot of time visiting with May.

Angel felt guilty that during the last few weeks she had not spent that much time with May. Jake meant a lot to May and she probably grieved in solitude. It had probably put more of a strain on her aunt than any of them had realized. Although each was dealing with their grief in their own way it seemed, May was the only one who had gone through most of it alone.

When the ceremony was over and all the condolences were done, Angel and her girls made their way home. Another funeral was wearing on Angel and the girls, but once again Tanya was at the rescue.

Entering her kitchen, Angel found Tanya preparing a casserole for the oven. "Tanya, you are a godsend. I don't know what we would ever do without you. Thank you so much for being here. These are such trying times and I know that you have your own trying times."

Tanya popped the casserole in the oven and removed the oven mitts. "May lived a good and full life, but I know how much you and the girls are going to miss her. I'm going to miss her wit, always knew what to say to set you straight, or brighten your day."

"Yes, that was Aunt May's way, wasn't it? She pulled no punches when she wanted to make her point."

Tanya sat at the counter and Angel joined her. "Would you like a cup of tea, Angel?"

"No. You've done enough and I'm fine."

"What will happen to the manor, will you put it on the market?"

"I probably will, yes. But right now there's just too much heartache to make anymore decisions for the time being."

Tanya patted her hand. "Well, I guess I'll be on my way. Bob is probably wondering when I'm coming home."

Angel smiled and stood up. "It's so great to have family like you. You're very much like Jake in many ways." She hugged her sister-in-law.

"Oh, I almost forgot. Rachael mentioned this morning that she might not be going to Truro to the Agriculture College. What's going on with her?"

"She's supposed to leave this weekend. She has to be there by Monday. Is that all she said?"

"It was just a passing remark on her way out the door." Tanya gave Angel another hug and hurried out the door back to her husband. Angel watched her drive away and suddenly felt concerned about Rachael, wondering why she would say such a thing.

The girls had gone up to their rooms after the funeral, and when Angel reached the top of the stairs she knocked on Rachael's door then entered.

"Hi. What are you up to?"

Rachael was standing in the middle of the room listening to music on her iPod. She turned when Angel entered the room. "Hi, Mom. Just going out to get some rays. Why don't you put on your swim suit and join me at the pool? I think we need some R and R, don't you?"

"Are you finished packing?"

"Well, I've done a lot. Still a few things to do."

"Rachael, what's this I hear about you might not be going to college?"

"Who told you that?"

"Tanya mentioned that you said something on the way out of the house today."

Rachael put down her iPod and slumped on the bed. "I...I just don't feel up to it."

Angel sat beside her daughter. "But, you're almost ready. You never mentioned anything to me about having second thoughts. It's your second year, Rachael, how can you not go?"

"I won't be able to concentrate. Maybe I can go late, or next year."

"And what would you do for a whole year?"

"Work in town at the vet clinic, or maybe volunteer at the SPCA."

"Rachael, you know that doesn't make sense. Go out to the pool, yes, and relax and think about what you're saying. But, no, it's not the right decision to put this on hold." Angel got up and left the room.

Rachael sat on the bed wondering what to do next. How could she concentrate on studying? Her dad was dead, her aunt was dead. What a summer it had turned out to be. Rachael didn't feel like doing anything. Her first thought was to run to her cubby hole, but then she thought of Aunt Tanya. Rachael grabbed her car keys and ran down the stairs.

"Rachael? Where are you going?" Angel asked.

"I'll be right back, Mom, but if I'm not, don't wait supper for me."

"Rachael!" Angel stuck her head out the front door but her daughter was already in her car and halfway down the long driveway.

CHAPTER FIVE

Rachael ran up the pathway to the large Cape Cod style house, where her Aunt Tanya and Uncle Bob lived. She pushed open the front door and bounded through the living room calling, "Aunt Tanya, where are you?"

Rachael saw the patio doors open and rushed through them to the garden beyond. Her aunt and uncle were seated at a round, white table having supper.

"Rachael. What are you doing here?"

Rachael felt like an intruder. "I'm sorry, Aunt Tanya, but I just had to talk to you. Mom's getting on my case about going to college. I…I don't know what to do."

Tanya made a spot for Rachael to sit. "Can I get you a plate?"

"No, I told Mom I'd be right back. I just need you to tell her that I can't go back to school. She'll listen to you. Please, Aunt Tanya."

Tanya scowled. "Rachael, you know I can't do that. And besides, I agree with your mother. Getting on with your life and getting back into your studies will be the best thing for you right now. I'll be here for Angel and Mae if that's what you're worried about. I'll check on them often and I'll email you. Okay?"

Rachael's lip quivered. "I'm scared, Aunt Tanya, what if I can't concentrate, what if I can't keep up?"

Bob had been sitting quietly, but he now spoke up. "Maybe it's none of my concern, Rachael honey, but your Aunt Tanya's right on this one. You can't stop your life just because these awful things have happened to you. Think about your dad and how proud he was of you. He bragged about you all the time, always telling me how great you were doing and how much you loved animals and what a wonderful veterinarian you were going to be. Can you let him down now?"

Rachael looked at both her aunt and uncle and blinked her eyes. She thought deeply about what they had said. "I…I guess I never thought about Dad and what he would think. I know he'd tell me to get my butt back there, there was work to be done." Rachael smiled just thinking about her father.

Tanya and Bob both laughed. "That he would," Tanya agreed. "So Rachael, get your butt back there."

Rachael jumped up and hugged her aunt and uncle. "I gotta get home, Mom's expecting me. Thanks guys. I guess I'll see you at Thanksgiving if not before."

Tanya stood up and placed her arms around her niece. "Take care, Rachael. You'll do fine. And write me."

"I will."

Rachael hurried home to tell her mom the news that she was indeed going back and not going to disappoint either her father or her mother.

****

The manor looked forlorn as Angel drove up and pulled a for sale sign out of her trunk. She found a hammer in the shed and pounded the sign on the front lawn. Turning, she gazed at the front porch, expecting any minute to see Aunt May swing open the screen door and holler, "Yoo-hoo." But there was only silence looking back at her.

Angel stood back and looked at the sign. It was only homemade and might not do the trick, but if there were no responses to the property, she would let a real estate agency handle it. She didn't want to sell the manor, but she couldn't keep it. It would only go downhill and she didn't need two houses.

The fall had been a lovely one, with so many beautiful warm days. Angel walked up to the manor door and went inside. She stood in the long hallway and listened to the silence. So much to do. All of May's worldly possessions to pick over and decide what to do about.

Instead of starting at the cleaning and sorting, Angel ventured upstairs and into the small bedroom that had been hers when she'd come to the manor sixteen years earlier, back when it was a vibrant Bed and Breakfast. It was a store room now of sorts, packed almost ceiling high with boxes and items from the house that May no longer used. Angel got a chill while standing in the humid air. She made her way through the boxes and decided to start at the closet.

She found some of her Aunt May's old clothes and a few old-time hats on the shelf. Angel tossed them onto the floor in the only clear space she could find. She reached far back on the closet rod and pulled forward an old dress. She smiled. Why it was the old outfit she had worn on the plane the day she'd arrived. She recalled telling her Aunt May that she would be wearing a long white dress, with a floppy hat and carrying a red purse. This was for Jake's benefit when he came to pick her up, as Angel was not sure he would know her.

Holding the dress at arm's length, Angel marvelled at how it still looked good, although it had yellowed slightly. The big floppy hat lay on the top shelf with more old ones of May's, and it looked just the same as the day she had worn it on the plane.

On an impulse, Angel stepped out of her shorts and tank top and pulled the long dress on. She grabbed the hat and headed out into the hall to gape at herself in the full-length mirror. Shockingly, she discovered that she was even thinner now than she had been when she had worn the dress all those many years ago. She stuck the floppy hat on her head and walked down the stairs and out into the front yard.

Following the path that led to behind the manor and out into the orchard, Angel noticed that the trees were loaded with apples this year. When she reached a corner in the path and spied the old tree with the low limb that hung like a seat, Angel's eyes misted in memory of that day so long ago, when she and Jake had strolled the same path. She seated herself on the limb and stared at the old deserted barn.

This was where Jake had first asked her to go golfing with him, and when she had balked remembering how her first husband, James, had embarrassed and ridiculed her when they had played golf. Finally Jake had convinced her and she had gone golfing with him, after some prodding from Aunt May. It had all turned out so lovely that day, and that was the day that Angel realized Jake was nothing like her former husband, James.

Sitting quietly, Angel glanced at the old barn, which was even more entangled with tree limbs and creeping woody plants than before. She closed her eyes and listened to the breeze rushing through the trees. It reminded her of an ocean wave crashing on the shore then receding, only to crash again. The soft songs of the little birds and the harsh penetrating call of the brassy crows were music to her ears. She had never felt so peaceful since Jake's death than she felt at that moment. When she was there at the manor, she was home, home in her heart. How could she sell it?

Thinking of the for sale sign out on the front lawn, Angel jumped from the tree seat and stomped from the orchard to the front of the manor. She yanked on the sign, pulled it towards the ground and let it drop.

That was it. She couldn't sell the manor. There were too many wonderful memories there, with her and Jake and her loving and straight-talking Aunt May. With the sign down, Angel burst into tears and ran back into the orchard. She cuddled up under the big tree, leaning her back against its mighty trunk and thought.

Her eyes were planted firmly on the backside of the old barn. It would make a great workshop. People could paint and write in solitude on the beautiful grounds and stay in the manor, where they could collect their thoughts and dreams and work their creativity to the bone.

"A retreat," Angel shouted to the sky. "What better way to commemorate the memory of both Jake and Aunt May?" Suddenly she could see it, Angel's Retreat, a big sign, as artists and writers drove up the long tree-lined lane. She could picture it all, what a place! She had to do it. She had helped her aunt so many times, while her aunt had been running the Bed and Breakfast. She had gotten quite good at serving and greeting guests and she liked it a lot.

She had also developed her own art business, and for a while she ran a small art gallery and store in Apple Grove. She gave it up only after her daughter, Mae, was born, and she then became a stay-at-home artist/mom.

Her head was spinning. There was so much to do. She assumed there would be people that would scoff at her idea but she didn't care. She was going to sell a house all right, but the house would not be the manor. She took the sign down because the manor now had a new owner. Angel Jordan, Proprietor.

Leaving the orchard behind, Angel hurried up the path to the front of the manor. She slipped through the screen door and stood in the hallway. Looking around at all the rooms, she knew there would be quite a renovation going on. And she needed help. If only Jake were here. He'd be able to give her advice, and he knew so many people in the area that finding a good contractor would have been simple for him.

Angel had a lot to do. The house that would be sold would be their house, the one that she and Jake had lived in all their married life. She loved the house but it was too empty now, with Rachael away at college and with Jake gone. There were too many memories in that house, and she wasn't feeling comfortable living there anymore.

But what to do? Who to call? Maybe Tanya would have some ideas, or Bob. Then for some reason, William Canton popped into Angel's mind. He was, or had been a businessman. He probably knew tons of people in the area. She shook her head, wondering why he even came into her mind.

It was strange but when she'd talked with him at the park, she felt something that was akin to closeness. It was foolish, yes, to even think such things, but if she were to be truly honest with herself, talking to William Canton had made her feel close to Jake.

Yes, foolish…and crazy. She felt like he might be the only person that she could really talk to about Jake and feel that he understood her pain. For he was going through some guilt himself over the accident, she could tell by the way he looked at her.

In all probability he could offer her some sound business advice. But even if he objected to whether it might be a good business venture or not, Angel was prepared to state her case and let him know that she was only asking for business advice, and he could keep his personal opinion to himself.

Angel decided to close up the manor for now and go home. She had a lot to think about. At home she searched her landline phone for William Canton's number. She knew he had called her from the hospital and his number must still be on there. All she had to do was look for that fatal day when Jake had died and sort through the numbers.

Scrolling through the August 16th phone calls, it didn't take Angel long to find the unfamiliar number. She decided there was no time like the present and hit re-dial.

After four rings she was just about to hang up when a click brought a hello from the voice that she remembered as William Canton's.

"Hello, Mr. Canton. This is Angel Jordan. I'd like to have a few words with you if you don't mind."

"Mrs Jordan, I do believe I've told you all that I remember about the day in question."

"No, no. This is not about that."

"Oh?"

"No. And I hope you won't find me forward in asking you this, but from what I know of you, you and my husband were business associates of sorts, is that right?"

"Well, we knew each other as I was in land development also. There were times when we were rivals as well."

"It's strange that he never spoke to me of you."

"I lived in Halifax for years, Mrs Jordan. And it's not like we were personal friends then. When I moved to the Valley we did golf together some."

"I see."

"What seems to be on your mind?"

"Well, it's business related and I'd rather not discuss it on the phone. I'd rather talk face to face if you would have some time for me…at your convenience of course."

"It sounds rather intriguing, Mrs Jordan. But as you might know, I'm no longer in business. I do some consulting, but I've taken early retirement and spend most of my days on the lake."

"Well, it won't take much of your time."

"Let me get back to you."

Angel had hoped to settle up a meeting today, but she took a deep breath and realized that she must be patient. She didn't think Mr. Canton was a man that could be hurried. "That's fine, Mr. Canton. I hope it won't be too long."

"I'll be back to you in a day or so."

"Good. We'll talk then. Good day."

Angel put the phone down. Her mind was full of dreams of the future. A pang of guilt seeped into her head at the thought of even thinking of the future, when just yesterday she was still lost in a fog so deep. Did she have the right to be making plans with Jake so freshly in the grave?

****

Angel was in the kitchen making a pizza when her phone rang. It had been three days since she'd talked with William Canton and every time the phone rang she had thought it would be him, but it wasn't. She had just about given up on him.

36

"Coming," she said, wiping her hands on a dishtowel. Grabbing up her phone, she said, "Hello, Angel Jordan here."

"Hello, Angel Jordan."

The voice was unmistakable. None other than the tardy Mr. Canton. "Oh, my, I didn't think I'd ever hear from you again. I thought you'd gotten cold feet."

She heard a laugh and it was a nice laugh. "Sorry to keep you dangling, but I had personal business that took me out of town. I just got back and figured I'd better give you a call. When would you like to meet and where?"

"How about the same place? It seems quite private there and nice. That is unless it's raining when the day comes."

"Well, I can meet you tomorrow, and as far as I know the weather is not going to be bad."

"Perfect. How about two-thirty or so?"

"My schedule is open and that sounds fine to me."

"See you tomorrow then."

"Tomorrow," he repeated.

Angel put her phone down and wondered just what she should be asking of him anyway. He was a total stranger, connected only by one bad event. She hoped he might be able to help her or give her a few names of people that could.

When she thought about it and how big a project it would be and how she knew squat about running a retreat or what she would need, or how she should renovate, Angel's heart raced. But she cautioned herself to calm down and see what tomorrow produced. She hoped it would be worthwhile.

¶

****

The sun was high and hot when Bill drove into the park. Angel Jordan was once again waiting on the park bench. This time she rose and walked towards his car.

She greeted him. "Hello, Mr. Canton, thank you for coming."

He noticed she even had a smile for him. Had she decided to forgive him for being with Jake the day he died? "Aren't we being just a bit formal? You can call me Bill, you know."

"Well, then you can call me Angel."

He smiled. "Would you like to walk today? My leg is feeling much better."

"Sure, let's walk up the path where it's cooler."

"I'm anxious, you know, to hear about your proposition or whatever. You did say it was business, didn't you?"

"Yes, it is." They'd reached another bench in the shade and Angel stopped by it and sat down. "I'll get right to the point. A while back, I visited my aunt's manor about to gather up her belongings and put a for sale sign on the lawn. In fact, I even did put the sign up, and I went inside to start packing up her things.

"But something distracted me and I took a walk in the orchard instead. While sitting there in the beauty of it all, I got this fantastic idea, or I think it's fantastic. You might not agree, but what I want from you is not your personal opinion, but rather a business opinion of what you think."

"I'm all ears."

"Good. So while sitting there gazing at the backside of the old barn on the property, I envisioned what it all could become. I want to open a retreat for writers and painters."

Bill was taken aback. He never expected to hear this kind of proposal, but he didn't know anything about Angel Jordan, so he kept an open mind. "Well, I'd say that's rather ambitious. Are you a writer?"

"No, but I'm an artist. And I think it would make a lovely retreat. There's nothing like peace and quiet in order to create, and I think I have what it takes to make it work."

"I admire your determination and your courage, Angel. What do you want from me?" He watched her fidget with her hands, turning the wedding ring that she still wore. She looked down at the ground seemingly grasping for words. He wanted to make it a little easier on her, so he continued, "What I mean is, what can I do for you?"

"Just what kind of friends were you and my husband?"

He was not expecting that come back. "I told you before, we were business associates, sometimes rivals, but we respected each other's territory and we sometimes played golf together. That was after I'd moved to the Valley. I've only been here a couple of years."

"So you said previously. Considering that, perhaps you don't really know a lot of people around here. Maybe you can't help me."

"Oh, I know a considerable amount of people. The Valley is not that far from the city. We're not all that out of touch, especially these days of the Internet, digital marketing and online businesses. I have an online business of my own as a business consultant, so I guess you've come to the right guy."

Angel looked up and smiled. "That's good to know. I hope you don't intend to charge me for your professional expertise."

"Never. Jake was a friend of mine, anything I can do for his lovely widow, I'm at your beck and call."

"Thank you, Bill. I'll try and not impose on your generosity too heavily. What I need to know are statistics. I'm wondering if such a venture would be appropriate for this area, and whether my idea, however exciting to me, would be worthwhile or not."

"It probably depends on whether this venture is something you want to turn into financial gain, or would be content to have it just stay afloat. I'm not saying that you won't make money, it's entirely possible, but is that your motive?"

"Definitely not. I am quite financially well off as you might imagine, being Jake's wife. He was not a man to leave any stone unturned."

"Then this is a venture of the heart?"

"You could call it that. It excites me and I think I need something like that right now."

"So you'll be looking for contractors as well? That is if my research turns out to show a need for such a business in this area."

"Yes, I will. I'll be looking for as much help as I can get from someone like you who seems to know the ropes."

"It does sound exciting. I don't know much about art myself, but I've written a few poems and short stories in my lifetime. And I find the peace and quiet of my cabin on the lake to be, as you said, essential for a creative outlet."

"That's wonderful, Bill. I didn't realize that you had a creative side, but then I know very little about you."

"We'll have to change that, Angel. Look, it's a great day and my boat is calling to me. Fish for supper perhaps. So if you don't mind cutting this short, I promise to get back to you with some information as soon as I can."

Angel sighed. "You don't know how relieved I am and how grateful. I know we didn't get off to a good start when we first met, but they were under awkward and harrowing conditions."

"You don't have to apologize for anything, Angel. I'm on the same wave length with you when it comes to our earlier conversations. I know where you're coming from. I can't change what happened that day in the car. I can't go back and rent a car and therefore let Jake stay in the Valley that day. I would if I could, but I can't. I can only go forward, much like yourself and everyone else on this planet. But I want to make it up to you, what I might have caused to happen…if I can."

Angel looked stressed and he wished he'd kept his mouth shut. She was just so damn easy to talk to. "Let's not go there, right now, Bill. Like you said, let's forge ahead. I look forward to hearing from you and hope you have good news for me." She shot a hand towards him and he felt obligated to shake it.

She turned and headed down the path and he followed a little way behind, his leg was hurting and he saw no need to keep up with her. She reached her car then paused, waiting for him to catch up. As he reached where she stood, she got in her car and drove away without another word. Bill got in his own car and drove towards the lake, looking forward to spending the rest of the afternoon in his boat, contemplating this very interesting meeting with one Angel Jordan.

CHAPTER SIX

While driving home, Angel was in good spirits. Her meeting with Bill Canton went well, she thought. He seemed like a very calm and thoughtful person. She hoped that he could find the information she was seeking for her business venture. For now she would wait until she heard from him.

Being in a good mood, she decided to have supper on the patio. It was such a lovely day and with Rachael gone, she wanted to do something nice for Mae.

When Angel got home, Mae was already there. "Hi, darling, how was your day?" she asked.

Mae was sitting on the veranda playing with her cat, Amber. "It was okay."

"How would you like to take a swim with me?"

Mae looked up interested. "Really?"

"Sure, why not, we're not going to have many more of these beautiful days to use the pool. Let's make a day of it. After our swim we'll cook hotdogs."

Mae's face lit up and she jumped up quickly, sending the yellow-orange cat off her knee and landing on its feet like all cats do. "I'll go up and get my swimsuit on. I want the big noodle."

Angel laughed, "You can have it. I plan to get some strokes in." She was glad that Mae seemed excited. She knew that she'd done very little with her daughter in the last month or so. It was time to get back to the world of the living. She looked up. "I'm trying, Jake. I'm trying to live the way you always did, in the moment. But I miss you."

She wiped a tear away with the back of her hand and told herself, no more tears today. She went up to her room and donned her swimsuit, realizing as she looked in the mirror that she had indeed lost a lot of weight.

****

Bill Canton called Angel three days later. He told her he didn't have all the statistics together yet. The weather had been so good that he'd been spending as much time as he could on the lake, but he'd found out enough to know there was nothing like that in the area and that was a good sign.

Angel was excited. "I really appreciate this, Bill. Really, I'm not in that big of a hurry, so take your time. I was just saying to my daughter, Mae, the other night that we had better take advantage of these nice days to get in some pool time."

"I'll keep looking and let you know what turns up. Although you made it clear that my personal opinion didn't count, I think it sounds like a great venture. I think it might be just what someone like you needs."

"What does that mean, someone like me?" Angel was slightly taken aback.

He laughed. "Only that you're very personable and artistic as well. You should do well with this."

Angel felt better. It had almost felt like he had been delving into her inner being for a minute. Her sensitive side was showing and she quickly remarked, "Oh. Then thank you, I guess. You'll call me when you find out more?"

"I'm going to talk to a few people around, some contractors, business people, see what kind of reaction I get."

"Okay, good. Let me know, and enjoy your fishing."

"Thanks, Angel. Maybe you might want to join me someday. Do you fish?"

Angel felt weird. She remembered her days on Jake's sailboat. She replied, "I did enjoy it…once."

After her conversation with Bill, Angel couldn't seem to concentrate on much else. The idea of her retreat was taking form, for she had decided to go through with it whether Bill Canton and his business friends thought it was a good idea or not.

****

With Rachael arriving home for Thanksgiving weekend, Angel tried to make the house festive. She got Mae in on it and being the artistic people that they were, it wasn't long before a fall festive theme had invaded the house.

Mae was excited to see her sister again, and Angel couldn't wait. Their parting in September had been a sombre one, with Rachael unsure of her future plans but willing to forge ahead anyway.

Rachael parked her belongings by the door and traipsed through the living room. She stopped in front of the fireplace and looked up at the painting of herself that Angel had painted when she was four years old. The mantel was adorned with leaves and fall colours. "I see you two have been busy. The house looks great, and it's so good to be home." Rachael sat down and sighed.

Angel smiled at Rachael and sat beside her on the sofa overlooking the pool. "We tried. I know it's been a tough time all around but I hope we can have a happy Thanksgiving. Your uncle and aunt are coming over for dinner."

"Cool. I can't wait to see them, How's Uncle Bob doing?"

"He's much the same. I think he was relieved when Tanya was not running over here every day to tend to my needs."

"You seem so much stronger, Mom. It makes me happy to see that."

Angel sighed. "Life goes on. And then there's Mae. I need to keep up for her also. She's a little girl and she needs my attention now more than ever before."

"Well, she seems to be doing okay."

"She is. She's doing great. You know Mae she's always been the quiet one. She has her father's stamina but she's not as outgoing as he was. She has some of my artistic hermitness I guess, if that's a word."

"Mom, I've never known you to be a hermit. Did Aunt May's house sell? I asked you a couple of times in emails but you never mentioned it."

"That's because it's not on the market right now. I just closed it up."

"Why?"

"Well, I'm not ready yet to make any decisions."

"Well, you made me make one, to go back to school."

"I didn't make you, Rachael, I suggested."

"Actually it was Aunt Tanya and Uncle Bob who convinced me that I needed to continue on with my life in the path I'd chosen. Now when I think about it, what good would it have done for me to mope around here? It certainly wouldn't have brought Dad back."

There was a moment of silence and Angel didn't want to dwell on the past. She knew there'd be time to talk about Jake and she wanted to with Rachael, but it wasn't now. "You made the right decision, Rachael," Angel said. She patted her daughter on the leg, gave her a hug and got up from the sofa. "It's such a nice day, do you want to spend some time in the pool? Last time this year."

"I know. Do you think it's warm enough?"

"It's a warm day but I have the heat on. The nights are chilly and they cool the water off, and the day's sun can't warm it enough to be comfortable."

Angel and Rachael went back to the foyer and carried Rachael's luggage up to her room.

Angel remembered Rachael's inquiries about the manor, and she purposely had neglected to talk about it. She was not ready yet to reveal her intentions for the manor, and later if things progressed as planned in Angel's mind, there would be the revelation about selling the house they now lived in. She wondered how both her daughters would take that bit of news.

****

By the end of October with no word from Bill Canton, Angel gave him a call. "Hello, Bill. How have you been?"

"Angel, I was just thinking about you."

"Oh? Is that a good thing?"

Bill laughed. "Of course. You're always pleasant to think about. And on my boat I do some of my best thinking."

"That boat must be a great place to be this fall. I can't get over the beautiful weather we've been having."

"I'm afraid it's all going to come to an end before long and we'll be in for a long, cold winter, although winter doesn't faze me. I have my snowmobile up here at the lake and there's always winter fishing."

"You sound very positive. Your lake sounds like a wonderful place to be."

"Maybe you'd like to come up someday and see where I live. If it's soon we can take the boat out."

"It sounds lovely."

"I guess you're wondering why you never heard from me."

"Yes, I was kind of expecting more news before now."

"I'm just a lazy bugger sometimes. You did tell me there was no hurry."

"Well, yes, but—"

"Hey, you're impatient. I get you. I have a few figures you might want to look at and some stats. Would you like to drive up to the lake and pay me a visit?"

Angel had not expected this. She was caught in a question that she had no answer for. "I...I don't know. You'd have to give me directions I guess and I'd have to think about it."

"If it's a problem I can meet you at the park."

"No," Angel answered quickly. "I just need some time. Can I call you back?"

Angel put the phone down and stared at it. Her hands flew to her face and she drew in a long breath and expelled it. "Wow," she said out loud. "What do I do now?" Why it was such a big deal, Angel had no idea. Why was going to Bill Canton's house on the lake something that hit her like a cannon ball. After all she had asked him for help, and he had obliged. They weren't total strangers anymore.

She started to think about what he had told her about the lake. The beautiful sunsets, the peace and quiet, the call of the loon. What a great place to paint it must be. Angel scoffed at herself. This was ridiculous. She'd love to see the lake and she'd love to go fishing again. But for now, it was business and she wanted to see the stats that Bill Canton had come up with. She called him back.

"Hi, made up your mind?"

"Definitely. I'd love to come to the lake."

After Bill gave her driving directions, Angel said she could make it tomorrow if that was okay. Bill said it was perfect as the good weather was supposed to continue into the weekend.

Friday morning Angel sent her daughter off to school then did up her household chores. She dressed in jeans and decided to take a heavy sweater along with her. She didn't know what to expect. It would be almost lunch time when she got to the lake, if she didn't get lost along the way. Would he ask her to stay? She would wait and see. Lately, she had decided to adapt some of Jake's spontaneity for life. It was one of the characteristics she had always loved about him.

Angel had no trouble finding the lake and Bill's house. It was actually a cabin, a beautiful log cabin, all cedar with a log veranda on the front. She parked her car beside Bill's and walked towards the house. She stood on the veranda and listened to the wind rush through the trees. The trees were tall around the cabin, pine and spruce, towering above it like giant sentinel watchers. They swayed in the breeze, some topped with jaunty black crows who acted like they owned them.

The veranda had white wooden lawn chairs, two placed together with a small wooden table in between. A white wooden lawn swing sat on the other side of the veranda. There were a number of plants as well; they all looked vibrant and well cared for. Mr. Canton had a green thumb as well. She turned when the screen door swung open and she was greeted by Bill.

"You made it." He laughed and to her surprise he reached out and gave her a hug. "Come on in. I just made lunch. It's that time of day you know."

Angel entered the cabin with Bill at her heels. The kitchen was fully equipped with all the necessities in appliances, very modern looking. Angel's eyes strayed to the open concept area which included the living room, with windows all around. No curtains adorned the windows, just wooden blinds all fully opened to let in the stream of sunlight that landed across the shiny pine floor.

The table was oblong with four chairs surrounding it. A lunch of sandwiches and fruit was on the table. In the far corner of the living area stood a black, Franklin type wood stove; the long, black stove pipe climbed up the wall and out the side. Across the front windows, a black leather sofa stretched out with pine tables at each end of it. Across from that, a large TV was on the wall. The walls were log and above it all was a sprawling cathedral ceiling.

"Well, you certainly have spared no comfort here, have you?"

"I like fishing on the lake, but I'm no pioneer. I enjoy modern conveniences." He motioned to Angel to sit down, as he pulled a chair out for her at the table. I've made coffee but if you prefer tea—"

"Coffee sounds great." Angel watched as Bill walked to the cupboard and retrieved the coffee pot. He was wearing jeans and a T-shirt that said,

I'd rather be fishing.

Bill poured the coffee, sat the pot on the table on a pot holder and looked at Angel. "Dig in. It's not fancy but then you're not here to sample my gourmet food are you?"

Angel laughed and reached for a sandwich. "I'd like to see those figures you told me about."

"And I'll be glad to show them to you." He reached to the end of the table for a pile of papers. "I think you're going to be pleasantly pleased."

Angel took the papers and scanned through them. She stopped at the third one. "You've compiled a list of writers and authors in the province."

"Well, yeah, just for data but I know you want to reach out to the world on the Internet. Are you any good with web design?"

"I mess around but nothing serious. What did you have in mind?"

He grinned. "I'm pretty good with it and if you'd like I can put a webpage together for you, just a sample of what you might like."

Angel put the papers down and looked in his eyes. "Bill, you amaze me. Is there anything you can't do?"

He threw his head back and laughed exuberantly. "Oh, you flatter me, Angel. But really it's not a big deal. And yes, there are plenty of things I can't do. Obviously, I'm not very good at keeping a wife."

Angel thought he had a very nice laugh, but the last thing that had come out of his mouth surprised her. Where was she supposed to go with that? Deciding to ignore his comment rather than delve into asking what he meant, Angel moved on. "Well, I'd be pleased for you to mock up a webpage for me, if it's not too much trouble."

"Hey, I just told you, I love doing that stuff, not on a nice day like this mind you, but late at night, or when I don't have a good book to read."

"Don't you get lonely up here?"

"Never. The loons and birds keep me company. I even have a few woodland friends that drop by for a bite now and again."

"Like?"

Bill leaned back and sipped his coffee. He sighed. "Well, there's Jerry, he's the neighbourhood friendly chipmunk. He loves to raid the bird feeders, and right now he's stockpiling for winter, so I've made sure he finds a few nuts around to store away for a cold winter's day."

"You're a real nature lover, Mr. Canton."

"Oh, we're back to being formal again, Mrs Jordan?" Angel gave him a sideways glance, while a grin played on her lips. "Hey, getting back to the business at hand, I'm really impressed with what I've been able to dig up on retreats. And I don't see any reason why yours wouldn't do well."

"My sentiments exactly. And besides, even if I don't make a million, that's not what it's about."

"Yeah, I've gathered that." Bill got up and started gathering dishes.

Angel jumped up as well and carried her plate to the countertop. "That was a lovely lunch and this is some great information. I should take it home now and study it. I'm really getting excited about this venture. And I know it's a lot to do. Have you included any names and addresses of contractors in here?"

"Sure, there's a few there."

Angel started to gather up her purse and sweater, but Bill intervened. "Are you leaving so soon? Eat and run?" Angel looked flustered and he wished he hadn't sounded so flippant. "I...guess you have a busy day at home."

"Not really," Angel said.

"Then why don't you stay, come out on the boat. I did promise you some fishing."

Angel hesitated. She was of two minds, one was to go home so she could devour the information that Bill had given her, and to dream of her retreat taking form, and the other was to take a deep breath and just go with it. She went with it. "I didn't think you meant today, but yeah, I'd love to."

"We can't count on the weather holding for too long. Better make hay while the sun shines...or better put, get the fishing done now."

Angel laughed again. He was always putting his foot in his mouth it seemed to her, never knowing how she would take what he said. He was a cautious sort when it came to women, she could tell that. Almost as if someone, some woman had always been on the defensive with him, maybe his ex wife? Someday she would like to hear the story of how that marriage played out, that is if she ever got that close to Bill Canton to get personal.

"I can't stay out too long, my daughter is in school and although I don't mind her being home alone for a short period of time, I don't like to leave her alone too long."

"I understand, we'll make this a quickie." Was that a blush he saw cross Angel's face? It seemed that whatever he said today it was turning sexual, and he really didn't mean it to sound that way. "We can fish for about an hour, is that okay?"

Angel, glad he had made another turn around from his quickie remark, quickly replied, "That sounds just about right."

"Okay then." Bill rubbed his hands together while standing before her as if he was anxious to get going. "I'll just go out and gather some gear and you can trail along if you'd like."

It wasn't long before they were walking down a wood's path. Ahead, Angel could see the lake water sparkling in the sun. It dazzled her eyes and she donned her sunglasses.

They walked out to the boat and Bill asked Angel to climb aboard. He untied the ropes bounding the boat to the dock and jumped in. Angel was seated across from him as he started the motor and chugged out slowly.

"Low water here, we'll soon be into deeper."

It was peaceful just chugging along; the afternoon sun was high in the sky and warm on Angel's face. It brought back old sailing days to mind, she and Jake, Rachael, and later Mae as well. But this was not a day for reminiscing, so she settled back and went with the flow.

CHAPTER SEVEN

Angel was drawn back from her reverie when Bill gunned the motor and the boat splashed across the water. She dug her fingers into the sides of her seat and hung on as the waves leaped and fell under the boat causing a bucking sensation beneath her.

"Whoa…this is fun," Angel shouted over the roar of the motor. Bill gave her a glance and was wearing a big grin.

Before long they were in much deeper water and he relaxed the motor then killed it. He got up to throw the anchor over the side then joined Angel and handed her a fishing rod. "These are two of my best; they're ultra light for fishing rainbow trout. I hope you like trout."

"I do. I'm very much a fish person."

"Meaning you like to fish?"

"What I meant was I like to eat fish, but I do like to fish also although I've not done any lake fishing from a boat like this."

"I guess you're used to the big sailboat. Any plans for it? Or is that something you have put on the back burner for now?"

"Actually, I haven't thought about it. I suppose I will sell it. I never was much of a sailor on my own."

"What about the girls?"

"Rachael's a very good sailor, but she's away now and I don't think she'd have the time for attending to it."

"I hear she's at vet college."

"She's attending the Nova Scotia Agricultural College. She's in pre-vet…second year."

Bill got out a container and opened it.

"Is that our bait? What do we use for rainbow trout?"

Bill dangled a big juicy worm in Angel's face. "Some like to use synthetic bait, but I go for the old fashioned worm. Lots in my garden."

"This rod is really lightweight, you weren't kidding."

"Yep. And there's a reason. Those little guys have really keen eyesight. If the line's too heavy, they can see it. If they do see it they are less likely to bite, they're not stupid either."

"I see," Angel said, shaking her head up and down and manoeuvring a slippery worm on her hook.

Bill did the same and they threw their lines in the water. As they sat quietly enjoying the afternoon sun and the slight breeze, it could have been a day in early summer. A couple of times they both got bites, but it seemed the trout were smarter than usual and when Bill turned the boat for shore, they went home empty handed.

After Bill had moored the boat, he gave Angel a hand and she jumped out on the dock. "That was fun," she said, smiling up at him.

"Yeah, another great day on the water."

"And so what that we didn't catch any fish."

"I agree. It's more about the feeling of fishing than the catching."

They walked back to the cabin and Bill put his gear away. Angel went inside to retrieve her papers and purse. She had already donned the sweater when they had returned on the boat. She was standing at her car when Bill came out of the shed. "I'll look these over and we can talk some more about that website, if there's any info I can contribute."

"Of course. I'm going to need help from you," Bill said.

Angel looked at the crinkles that formed around Bill's eyes when he smiled. She had an idea. Not quite sure she should go with it or not, but she had been going for it all day so why stop now? "After I look all this over," she said to Bill, while smiling up at him, "we should get together then. How about having dinner at my house one night and we can discuss the website idea?"

Bill hesitated and Angel thought maybe she had gone for it too much, or too soon. But he came back with, "Love to."

Angel relaxed and opened her car door. "You'll be hearing from me...soon."

As she drove away she checked her rear view mirror to find him standing right where she'd left him, looking towards her car. He raised his right arm and gave her a wave. She tooted her horn and rounded a corner.

****

Angel was almost home when she glanced at the time. She was later than she'd expected to be. Their time on the water talking and fishing had lasted longer than she had expected. But it was such a pleasant time and Bill was gracious company. He didn't talk much when he fished and Angel was fine with that, just an occasional word or two here and there to be heard above the sounds of the lake birds and the lap of the water.

Now, she realized that Mae would be wondering where she was. She hoped to find her daughter up in her bedroom as usual drawing something. But as she entered the double doors to the foyer, Angel couldn't believe what was coming towards her.

An angry Mae made a beeline for her mother and almost knocked her down. "Where were you?" she screamed, while pounding her fists on her mother's chest.

Angel got hold of her daughter's arms and held them back. Mae was still young enough to control. She spun Mae around and looped her arms around Mae's body. Carefully she walked her to the sofa. By now Mae had calmed down some and turned to Angel and said, "I thought you had an accident. Why didn't you answer your phone when I called you?"

"I didn't know you called. I'm sorry I didn't check for messages."

"Where were you?" Mae looked up at Angel. Her face was distorted with swollen eyes and runny nose.

Angel hugged her close. "It's okay now, darling. I'm sorry, so sorry." She rocked Mae in her arms, feeling guilty and selfish. How could she go off enjoying an afternoon and not think of her daughter? Why hadn't she called and told her when she'd be home? *You were enjoying yourself too much with William Canton.* The voice in Angel's head made her cringe.

Mae pulled from her. "Mommy, where were you?"

"I was...away, on business. And it took longer than I thought it would. I should have called you before leaving there, but I lost track of time. I'm sorry. It won't happen again, I promise."

Mae hugged her mother and said, "You promise? I thought you were dead, like Daddy."

"Oh, Mae, I'm right here. I will always be here for you. I won't leave you."

After the startling homecoming, Angel got Mae settled down and back to her normal self. They had supper together and Angel spent most of the evening with her. She wanted Mae to know that she was a first priority and promised herself never to do anything stupid like that again.

Later, when Mae was in bed fast asleep, Angel got the papers together and went into the living room. The night had turned chilly and Angel lit the fireplace. She cozied up in one of the big red leather chairs with a cup of Darjeeling tea and looked over the names of contractors and landscapers. She didn't know any of them, and she imagined that Jake would probably know at least some of them. But Jake was not here and she was lucky to have Bill Canton to help her out on her project.

Her mind wandered back to the afternoon. She had not allowed herself to think of it earlier, after Mae's reaction when she had got home. Now, she laid her head back against the cool leather, felt the heat from the fire and remembered the sun from the afternoon on the water.

No wonder Bill so enjoyed his life at the lake. Endless days of fishing and relaxing on the porch of that fabulous cabin, or just watching TV in that bright living room, it was magical.

But she had plans to make so she cleared her head of fantasies and went through the papers. One contractor looked as good as another to her, so she would have to rely on Bill's input and suggestion as to who might offer her the best service. She wouldn't be starting much until spring but there was inside work to be done now.

Angel felt tired and as she drifted off to a slumber, the papers sifted to the floor. The steam from her tea cup drifted lazily upward.

****

It had been quite an interesting afternoon. Bill Canton smiled to himself remembering almost everything about Angel. How she smiled, even how she wound that little slippery worm around in her fingers, almost expertly. He was proud of her for being as strong as she seemed. After all it was only a couple of months since Jake died. He had heard that she'd had a rough go of it for a while. But she seemed to be bouncing back remarkably. And she hadn't questioned him anymore on the accident. Still, it didn't lessen his feelings of guilt for the day Jake died.

He had really been shocked when she'd invited him to her house for dinner. She obviously liked him enough to spend the time at her house, rather than at some park or restaurant talking business.

He had never been to Jake's house. He had been past it several times. At one time he had even driven in the yard to pick up Jake when they were playing golf. He remembered that day. No one else had been around.

He wondered what he should take. A bottle of wine would probably be appropriate. He didn't even know if Angel drank. He knew so little about her, and there hadn't been much time today to learn more. But he assumed there would be time for that. And he hoped that if nothing else, he could help her out, get her business on the road, and maybe at the same time, both of them could deal with the guilt and misery of Jake's death and put it away for good.

Bill had just made up a roaring fire and stood beside it looking at the flames leaping high then falling. It always made him sleepy. And an afternoon on the lake always relaxed him, whether he caught fish or not.

****

It was early November when Angel finally got up the nerve to call Bill and ask him to come for dinner. She didn't know why she was so nervous. He was so easy to talk to and he never made her feel uncomfortable, but she was feeling uncomfortable now, and she didn't know why. It was a simple dinner invitation. He had invited her to his place and they had shared lunch together, was this any different?

Angel wondered what people would think. What would Tanya think? Would she be shocked to know that Angel had invited a man to her house only three months after her husband had died? Well, it wasn't like that. Mae would be there and she didn't expect Bill would stay that long. Have dinner, talk about the retreat project, try and firm up some contacts to get them into the manor and get started. Angel was anxious to get this thing off the ground.

She put her fears away and made the phone call. It rang a few times and she was just about to disconnect when she heard his voice.

"Hi, Bill. You keeping warm up there at the lake?"

He laughed. "Oh, I'm cozy. Weather has turned a bit colder, eh?"

"Well, it's to be expected, I suppose."

"So, what have you got on your mind, Angel Jordan?"

Angel had expected to move into the invitation slowly, but Bill was not one to dwell long on small talk. He was a to- the- point kind of guy, she was learning. "I was just thinking about our fishing expedition. And I wanted to thank you for such an enjoyable afternoon. So, I was wondering when you might be available to come to dinner."

"Hmm, I'm mostly free so you set the time and I'll be there with bells on."

Angel laughed. "I think you'll need to wear more than bells, it is a bit nippy out there."

"Okay, I'll leave the bells at home. Seriously, any time, you name it."

"I was thinking tomorrow night?"

"Tomorrow night sounds perfect to me. Can I bring anything?"

"No, I've got everything covered. Just bring yourself."

"I think I can manage that, and thank you. It's been a while since I've had a dinner invitation."

"You're welcome, Bill. I'll see you about six?"

"I'll be there. Looking forward to it."

Angel heard his phone click and stood in the middle of the living room looking around. She did it. She made the call and it was easy. Now, she had to plan what to have. She didn't know much about Bill Canton, except that he liked fish. But to have fish would be maybe going a bit too far. She'd have spaghetti with meat balls. Every red-blooded man she ever knew loved spaghetti with meat balls. She hoped that Bill was one of them.

Angel was lost in her thoughts when the front door opened and Mae walked in. Angel turned to greet her daughter. "Hi, Mae, how was school today?"

Mae hunched her shoulders. "Same as every other day, Mom, why?"

Before Angel had a chance to respond, Mae had taken up the stairs and to her room. Angel was once again brought back to reality. She would have to let Mae know they were having company. She went up the stairs behind her daughter.

Mae was already in her room, tossing her backpack on the bed and pulling off her jacket. "Mae, I'd like a word with you. Sit down here beside me."

Mae slumped down on the bed with a look on her face as if she had done something wrong.

"Tomorrow night we're having company for dinner."

"Aunt Tanya and Uncle Bob?"

"No. Someone you don't know. He's been helping me with my business."

"What business?"

"Well, business arrangements. Things I need to tie up and get done to move on with my life."

"You mean since Daddy died."

"Yes, something like that."

"Who is he?"

"Well, he's an acquaintance of your father's, and he's been in business so he offered to help me with a few things."

"Cool." Mae looked up at her mom and smiled. Her long red hair was tied back in a ponytail and her cheeks were pink from the outside air. "Is that all?"

"I…I guess."

"Pheww, I thought you were going to scold me over something."

Angel smiled and pushed back stray hairs on Mae's forehead. "Whatever for? It's not like you get into trouble. You're a very good girl and I appreciate it. It makes my job much easier."

Mae laughed. "Your mother job?"

Angel laughed too. "Yeah, being a mother is hard sometimes, but other times it's pretty nice, most of the time."

"Can I draw now?"

"Sure." Angel rose and walked to the door. She stopped and turned to glance at Mae already at her desk. She certainly loved to draw. Angel was glad that was over with, now on to the menu for tomorrow night.

****

The night was crisp and Angel jumped when she heard the doorbell. He was here. She pulled off her apron and went to the door. Opening it wide, she smiled. "Hi, Bill. Come on in."

"He was wearing a heavy charcoal pea jacket, which he immediately removed. "Boy, it's warm in here."

"I've got a blazing fire in the fireplace."

Angel took Bill's coat to hang in the closet. When she returned, he moved towards her. "Hello, Angel, it's so nice to see you again. And thanks for the invitation." He gave her a hug and as he pulled away, he retrieved a fancy bag that he'd placed on the entrance table when he'd arrived. "Just a little something. I hope you like wine."

Angel was taken aback by his warm hug, but after the greeting at the lake, she'd come to realize that Bill was an affectionate kind of person. He meant nothing by it except a friendly gesture. Angel took the wine. "That's great. We'll have it for dinner. Come sit. I'll pour us a glass right now."

As she left the living room to go to the kitchen, Angel noticed Mae standing on the bottom stair. Mae had a strange look on her face. Angel stopped. "Oh, Mae, come meet our guest. Mae, this is Bill Canton. Bill this is my youngest daughter, Mae."

Bill rose from the sofa and reached for Mae's hand. "Lovely to meet you, Mae. You're as pretty as your mother, and I see you've got her red hair too."

Mae stepped back, ignoring his outstretched hand. "Hi," she said, then wheeled around and left the living room, bounding up the stairs two at a time.

Angel gave Bill a look but he didn't seem to be bothered by Mae's quick disappearance. She wondered if Bill had children of his own. She again reminded herself that she knew very little about him. "I'll just get that wine," she murmured and turned towards the kitchen.

When she entered the kitchen, she was faced with an almost boiled over pot of spaghetti. Angel quickly removed it from the burner and turned the heat down. Everything else was ready, but the spaghetti would need her immediate attention unless she wanted a mess in the kitchen.

Bill took in his surroundings, it was a nice room. He especially liked the wood panelled walls and the fireplace with the rich wood mantel, which looked like it was probably walnut. Someone liked to read by the looks of the floor-to-ceiling bookcase with sliding glass doors, which took up all of one wall. Double windows made for an airy space. Bill thought the room would be very bright in the summer. The walls were sort of peach and the area rug was dark grey, a bit lighter than his pea jacket. He liked the room.

Angel poked her head out of the kitchen. "I'd say we're just about ready here. Sorry I never got back with the wine. Dinner took my attention."

Bill rose and walked through the hallway. Angel had returned to the kitchen and her back was to him. The cabinets were a dazzling white with charcoal granite countertops. The ceramic floor tile was white also. He did like a bright kitchen, and he loved the island in the centre of the floor, which right now was crammed with dishes and pots and pans.

"Anything I can do? I'm pretty handy in the kitchen."

Angel swung round, her face was flushed. "You can open the wine, please."

Angel proceeded to drag food to the dining room just off the kitchen. After Bill opened the wine, he took it to the table and poured two glasses, one for Angel and one for himself. He had no idea which seat he was sitting in, but he assumed he was to the side and Angel was at the end. Mae's plate was across from his, with a tumbler type glass instead of a wine glass.

Angel went to the stairway and gave Mae a call, then returned to the dining room. Bill picked up his glass and held it high. "A toast to you, Angel, an indomitable woman."

The glass Angel had earlier reached for shattered on the floor. Angel stood looking down in amazement.

Bill was speechless, unable to move. What had just happened here? He regained his momentum. "Are you all right, Angel?"

Angel still stood like stone, staring at the floor. Trickles of wine lay amongst chards of glass.

Bill took Angel's arm and backed her away from the mess. "I've got this. Where's your broom?"

Angel walked zombie-like to the living room, and Bill went into the kitchen and looked around. He saw two full-length closet doors. He tried one and found a wine display. In the other he found what he was looking for, the broom and dustpan. After sweeping up the broken glass, he mopped the liquid with paper towel, being careful not to get any tiny fragments in his hand. After he thought he had it all, he joined Angel in the living room.

Sitting beside her on the sofa, he noticed Mae, once again standing on the lower step looking into the living at her mother. Bill returned his attention to Angel who seemed to be recovering slightly.

"Was it something I said?"

Angel nodded. "Yes," she said in a meek voice. "It was the word, *indomitable.* Jake once told me that I was indomitable. We had been having a discussion about my ex-husband or something or other and it just came all crashing back to me."

Bill was at a loss for words. This little dinner party had certainly gotten off on the wrong foot. He felt as if he had stepped into the middle of something he was not prepared to handle. He didn't believe that Angel and Mae were up to their usual standards as far as hiding grief went. He understood it though and he would be cautious.

"Look, if this is a bad time, I can leave."

Angel came around. "No, no." Her hand flew up to touch his shoulder. "This is not your fault. You had no idea…and I'm making way too much of a word." She attempted a smile.

"I do understand. It was a moment, and I'm sorry for my choice of words."

Angel rose, followed by Bill. "Let's put this behind us, okay? Now come on, dinner is getting cold." Angel walked by the stairs and put her arm around Mae's waist escorting her to the table.

CHAPTER EIGHT

Although Angel tried to make jokes and keep the conversation light, Bill felt a bit uncomfortable. He wondered if it had been a good idea to come to dinner, after all he barely knew Angel. He also noticed that Mae was very quiet. He didn't know if this was her normal personality or if it was because he was there. Bill Canton was very tuned in to people's feelings. After all, his own mother had decided that he was the son she'd wished she never had.

When dinner was done and the dessert had been served, Bill thought it time to make a break in the general conversation. "What a great dinner, Angel. You've outdone yourself."

Angel laughed, seeming fully recovered from the earlier mishap. "Not really. Almost anyone can throw spaghetti together."

"Yes, but the apple pie is amazing."

"Aunt May taught me a lot about cooking and baking. She did run that bed and breakfast practically by herself most of the time, you know."

"I didn't know her, sad to say. But I'd heard lots about her from Jake."

Angel's face grew a cloud across it, but she tried to hide it. "Jake and May were very close."

The conversation seemed to come to an end, and Bill thought it was a good time to start talking business. "Did you get a chance to look over the list of contractors that I gave you?"

"I did, but I'm none the wiser. I don't know any of them."

"Would you like me to make a suggestion?"

"I'd be grateful."

Bill glanced at Mae, who was picking at her pie. "Rather boring conversation, isn't it Mae? But your mother and I have some business to attend to."

"So she told me," Mae replied, not looking up.

Bill felt a chill in the air, despite the heat in the house. He got up, pushed back his chair and placed his napkin on his plate. "Do you mind if we go over those names now, Angel? I really should be getting back home soon."

Angel rose as well and carried her plate to the kitchen. Bill did the same. Mae remained at the table, still concentrating on her pie. After offering to give Angel a hand in the kitchen, which she refused, Bill went into the living room to wait for her.

Angel wasn't far behind him with papers in hand. "I did an Internet search on the ones I could find, and these three sound pretty good." She sat beside Bill on the sofa.

Bill looked them over. He contemplated the names for a minute then replied, "Of these three, I would say Barre's Construction. I've known Jim Barre for quite a while. The company has a good reputation and they're a family business."

Angel smiled at him. "Okay. I guess I'll go with your expertise then."

Bill laughed. "If you're that trusting in me, I can recommend plumbers and electricians as well as a good landscaper."

Angel looked serious and took the papers from him. "I do trust you, Bill. You were a friend of Jake's, and any friend of Jake's is a friend of mine. I do need your help, but I don't want to impose."

"Nonsense. Not like I'm busy or anything."

"But you have your consulting work, and I don't want to take up your time."

Bill rose and stood before her. "I'm sure that once you get everything in place at the manor and the work begins, you won't have any trouble with the guys I'm about to recommend. However, I will be around to keep an eye on things with you. I've started this now and I'm not about to run out on you. It's been a great evening but I really must get going."

He walked back to the dining room to say goodbye to Mae but found that she was no longer at the table. "You have beautiful daughters, Angel. I look forward to seeing Rachael sometime as well."

"Rachael will be home at Christmas. Maybe you will get to see her then."

"Maybe."

Angel took Bill's coat from the closet and passed it to him. "Thanks so much for coming, Bill, and I'm sorry about the incident."

He winked at her. "What incident?"

He gave her a hug, then left.

****

As Angel cleaned up from dinner, the retreat was not the only thing on her mind. For some reason Bill's presence in her house and at her dinner table gave her an uncomfortable feeling. She wasn't sure it if had been because of the broken glass and that incident, or the fact that Mae had been so silent and cool during dinner. Or maybe it wasn't either of those things.

She scoffed at herself, otherwise happy that she now had some names and could get on with contacting the workers. She turned around from placing dishes in the dishwasher to see Mae. She was standing in the doorway of the kitchen staring at her mother.

Angel closed the dishwasher. "Mae, what's wrong?"

"Who was that man?"

"I told you, he's helping me with business. And I told you he was coming. You didn't seem to have a problem with it."

Mae sat on a stool at the kitchen island. "I know, but—"

"But, what?"

Angel joined her on another stool. Mae was looking down. "Well…before I went upstairs, I heard you two talking. And you were talking about the manor. I thought you were selling the manor."

"I changed my mind."

"Why?"

"Because I couldn't bear to part with it and because I'm thinking of doing something with it."

"What?"

Angel stopped to think how she would explain the situation. "Okay, I'll tell you. But promise you won't mention it to Rachael. I want to tell her myself when she gets home."

"Okay."

"Well, the manor is beautiful, right? And all that lovely land and orchards around it are as well. So, one day I got an idea to turn it into a retreat."

"What's a retreat?"

"Well, this one would be for artists and writers."

"Why?"

"Well, because, Mae, Mommy needs something to do now. Things have changed and I thought it would be a nice thing to do for Daddy and for Aunt May, they always loved that place, you know."

Mae got up and stood before her mother, her hands on her hips. "I don't think that's why you're doing it at all. I think you're doing it with that man, and I don't want him here again."

Angel couldn't believe what she was hearing. Her hand flew to her face. "Mae, that's not true. Bill is just helping me, because he knows business, much like your father would do, if he were here. Oh, darling, you're right, it's not just a way to remember your father and your Aunt May, but it's also for me. I need something right now. I need to do something that matters. Someday you'll understand…I hope."

Angel hugged her daughter, but Mae stood stiffly not responding. "I've got homework," she said and turned and went upstairs.

Angel stood in the kitchen, not knowing quite what had just happened and fearing the worst. How could she make her young daughter understand that she needed the retreat? Perhaps she could somehow get Mae involved in the project. After all, Mae was very artistic. Yes, she would include Mae and maybe she could get excited over the possibilities of what could be.

The next morning Angel wasted no time in contacting the people on the list that Bill had recommended. Of course none of them were available right then, but that was okay with Angel. She told them she wished to start early in the new year, and they agreed that something could be worked out.

With that she set the project aside. There was plenty to do before the workers arrived. She had to clean out the manor, perhaps a yard sale or two. Some things of course she would keep. The more she thought about it, the more she realized that there wouldn't probably be much that would leave the manor. She did want to replace some of the furnishings in the living room and perhaps update the kitchen, but it ripped her heart out to think of changing one single thing that Aunt May had owned there.

It would definitely be a country manor, and there were already new bathrooms installed from the bed and breakfast days. Angel knew she had her work cut out for her in the days ahead, and that her mind would be humming with thoughts of alterations.

She made a note to contact the contractor again to perhaps have a meeting and discuss the possibilities before construction began. Of course the old barn and the grounds would be the major construction. That old barn was like an empty shell, and Angel knew that definitely some design ideas were needed there.

During the rest of November, Angel busied herself with thinking about the retreat project, while she went through and disposed of May's belongings. It was a hard thing to do and there were days she couldn't bear to go to the manor and rummage anymore.

Angel had found old letters from her uncle to May, ancient birthday, anniversary and Christmas cards. There was a lifetime of her aunt and uncle's life in that house, and Angel saved a few special things, but the rest had to go. She would go to the manor and be home before Mae got home from school. She didn't want a repeat of what had happened when she had gone to Bill's cabin and Mae had gotten so upset.

By the end of November things were pretty well coming together, and Angel decided to stop visiting the manor until after Christmas. It wouldn't be long now before Rachael was home for Christmas break.

One morning in early December when Angel was in the kitchen preparing a fruit cake, Jake's sister Tanya stopped by for a visit. Angel grabbed a dish towel and wiped her hands and hurried to the door.

"Tanya, what a nice surprise, you don't get over enough."

Tanya gave Angel a hug. "I know, but lately Bob has been taking most of my attention. He seems to be getting worse, Angel." She had a worried expression on her face.

"Come in and have a cup of tea. I just made a cranberry loaf."

"Oh, that sounds delicious."

Tanya passed her coat to Angel who put it in the hall closet. She followed Angel into the kitchen and Angel proceeded to cut the loaf.

"I'm sorry to hear about Bob. It must be hard on you."

"It's harder on him I think. He thinks he's a liability."

"I'm sure you've put his mind at ease on that one, Tanya." Angel poured two cups of tea and sat with Tanya on the island stools.

"I try…but he sounds like a broken record. Says he wants to go into a nursing home, that it's too hard on me looking after him."

Angel laid her hand over Tanya's. This woman so like Jake, with the same brown eyes and dark hair. "Oh, Tanya, it would be hard on you to do that."

"What's hard on me is his attitude. I do everything I can for him, but he's gotten so negative lately. It's almost as if he's given up."

Angel didn't know how to console Tanya. "Love will find a way," she said, hoping what she had said would be enough.

"I don't think so, Angel. Every day is harder with him. But, never mind my troubles, what's going on with you?"

"Well, I've been cleaning out the manor, getting rid of some of Aunt May's belongings…a tough job."

"What about all that furniture? You going to have an estate sale?"

"Not just yet." Angel didn't want to mention her plans to Tanya until she'd had a chance to talk to Rachael, but it seemed that she didn't have to.

"Is it true then what Mae's been telling me, that you intend to keep the manor and turn it into some kind of retreat?"

Angel was caught; there was nothing to do but to explain things to Tanya. "Yes, Tanya, it is true. I just can't let the manor go. You know how much Aunt May loved it there, and you know the attachment Jake had to the place."

"Well, that may be true, but I just can't imagine you taking something like this on, Angel. How do you even know that it's a feasible thing to do?"

"Well, I've been consulting with other people and by the stats I've read, it seems there's nothing like it around here."

Tanya sipped her tea and eyed Angel. "Mae also told me that you and she had a dinner guest."

Angel laughed. "Oh my, Mae sure does like to gossip doesn't she?" Tanya sat quietly looking at Angel for a better explanation than that. "It was quite a while ago now, Tanya. One night I did have William Canton over for dinner. I had met with him on a few occasions earlier and invited him over for dinner so we could go over some business."

"What kind of business?"

"He's been helping me to find appropriate people to get my project started. You see, Bill is a business man, much like Jake was…that's how they happened to know each other."

"I know that."

"So, I thought of him when I needed some assistance in figuring out what contractor and other workers to get."

"Oh, I see. And that required a dinner date?"

"Tanya, it wasn't like that. It wasn't a date. What are you saying?"

"Nothing."

"Well, if you're insinuating that I am somehow involved with Bill Canton in other ways except business, then you are wrong. Not that it would be your business or anyone else's business if that were true."

"Don't get upset, Angel. I wasn't implying that at all."

"Good."

The kitchen was silent except for the humming of the kettle, which was still warm on the stove. Tanya sipped the last of her tea and rose. "I must get going. I guess it wasn't a good idea for me to visit when I was in a bad mood."

"Tanya, I know you're upset over Bob. I wish there was something I could do. After all, I won't soon forget all that you've done for me and the girls after Jake died."

"He was my brother, what else would I do?"

Angel gave Tanya a hug. "Don't worry about me or the girls. We've got ourselves together now. You need to concentrate on Bob. And if there's anything I can do to help out. Can I spell you once in a while so you can get out of the house and have some time to yourself?"

"Don't worry. I have a caregiver who does that for me. That's why I'm here. But I didn't mean to upset you."

"I'm not upset, okay? I am sensitive to your feelings when it comes to Jake and believe me, I would never disrespect them or Jake. Bill Canton is just a friend, and sometimes we all need one of those."

"That's true enough. I've gotta go, Angel. I have shopping to do and have to get back home soon. Take care and I'll see you at Christmas, if not before."

Angel watched her drive away and was still in shock when she thought of what Tanya had proposed. The thought of there being anything other than a business relationship between her and Bill was absolutely ridiculous. Angel was just about to go upstairs when her phone rang. She was actually surprised to hear Bill's voice.

"Hi, Angel. What are you doing on this beautiful day?"

"Oh, hi, Bill. What a surprise to hear from you."

"Really?"

"Yes, it is."

"I'm in town doing some errands and thought you might like to meet me for a coffee. I had a friendly call from Jim Barre the other night and he mentioned you. I told him I knew about your project and that I had recommended him for the job."

"I've decided to not work on the project too much until after Christmas. With Rachael coming home and Mae off for the holidays, it will be a busy time."

"I understand. He said you wanted to get started sometime in the new year. He hasn't worked out his schedule yet either. Anyway, want to meet me for a coffee at Tim's?"

Angel knew she had her fruit cake in progress, but after thinking about it, she decided she could use an ear to talk to. "I've been making fruitcakes, but I can meet you in about an hour. Is that too late?"

"Oh, no. I have things to do also. So see you later then?"

Angel hung up wondering if she was doing the right thing. They really didn't have any business to discuss right now as far as she knew. But she was feeling a bit down after Tanya's visit and thought some company might be good for her.

After she got her cakes settled away, Angel rushed out the door and down to the coffee shop. She saw Bill's car outside and he was standing beside it. "Hi," she called to him, walking towards him.

Bill met her half way and they walked to the coffee shop entrance. "November's turned out to be another good month, eh? I was tempted to stay home today and try my luck at fishing, but errands don't wait sometimes." He opened the door for her to go inside.

Just as Angel was about to enter, Tanya walked out through the door with a coffee in her hand. She looked from Angel to Bill and wore a startled expression.

Angel laughed. "We meet again, Tanya. Bill was just in town and asked me to have coffee with him." Tanya looked frozen in the doorway, so Bill opened it a bit wider. She stepped outside, and he let the door close. "Where are my manners? Tanya this is William Canton, a friend of Jake's, you might remember him from the funeral. Bill, this is Jake's sister, Tanya."

"I'd recognize you anywhere," Bill said. "You resemble him."

Tanya found her voice, but it wasn't a friendly one. "I've got to get going. Some of us have things to do." She hurried towards her car and Bill's mouth dropped open.

As they entered the coffee shop, he remarked," Well, I know one thing, she isn't nearly as friendly as Jake was."

After they got their coffee and were seated, Angel explained. "Tanya is going through a tough time right now, she isn't herself. Her husband is ill and he isn't getting better. She's been looking after him for years but things are starting to progress."

"What's wrong with him?"

"He has MS."

"I see. Must be tough then."

Angel didn't know what came over her but she blurted out, "And that's not the only thing that's bothering her today. I saw her earlier and she asked me why you were at my house for dinner. She seems to think there's something going on between us."

CHAPTER NINE

Bill was getting irritated. "So what?"

Angel leaned back, a surprised look on her face. "She's Jake's sister."

"Oh, yeah. And I'm the reason he's dead."

"I never said that, Bill. But Tanya is hurting a lot. You know I don't blame you."

"I thought you did…once."

"Once. Not now."

"Why the change of heart?"

Angel took a sip of coffee and looked Bill straight in the eye. "Just because Jake drove you to Halifax, it doesn't mean you made things happen. I'm sure you didn't want to lose a friend. It was just circumstances and I've come to terms with it. Tanya hasn't…yet. But she will eventually. She doesn't know you."

"And you do?"

"I think I know you somewhat, yes. You've been helpful to me and I enjoyed my time at your place, and the fishing. When I'm around you, Bill, I feel closer to Jake. I know that sounds stupid."

"Not stupid."

"I can't explain it any better, but—"

"I'm glad you feel that. It helps me too. Kind of takes the pressure off some, relieves the guilt."

"Oh, Bill."

Angel laid a hand across his, and Bill couldn't believe she had opened up to him this way. He didn't know whether to recognize the hand or to just take it as a gesture of sympathy or whatever. He decided to ignore it. "You know, aside from Jake's sister being here today, this little coffee date has become quite enlightening. It's not what I expected."

"I'm sorry. I don't know what came over me. You seem to have that affect on me. I feel like I can talk to you about anything, and I apologize for being so frank and forward."

It was Bill's turn to put a hand on Angel's, because she had just removed hers and was staring out the window, probably feeling embarrassed. "Angel, I don't want you to feel that way. You can tell me anything. Anything you want. This is a tough time for all of us, but especially you, and I would think that Jake's sister would have been more supportive of you getting on with your life."

"Is that what I'm doing?"

"Well, you've made plans for a retreat. I'd pretty much say that's getting on with your life."

"I think Jake would be happy for me."

"I do too."

"I hope Tanya will come around."

"I hope so too. But right now she's trying to tell you who to have and who not to have in your house."

"Mae told her."

"Oh. I noticed Mae was a bit quiet, but I thought maybe it was just her way. Look, Angel, if you're uncomfortable with me showing up at your house, we can meet somewhere else if we need to, or we can probably discuss most things on the phone." Angel was looking at him again, and when she looked directly into his eyes, it did funny things to the pit of his stomach that he wished would go away.

"I just told you, Bill, that I like talking to you. You have many good ideas and I'm sure more than I even know yet. If there are those that frown on me having you come to my house, then they will just have to get over it. I don't want to cause hard feelings between myself and Tanya. God knows I'd never want that to happen. She's been there for me though all of this, day in and day out for months, but this is her problem not mine. No one misses Jake more than I do, but I'm trying to live like he did. When Jake's first wife, Rachael's mother, died, he told me what he went through, but he came out of it for his daughter mainly. He lived for her...until I came along. I want to carry on his example."

"Well said, Angel. You do what makes you comfortable." Bill was himself feeling a bit uncomfortable right now. He was not a man for spilling his guts and he felt that if he stayed much longer, he might just do that. "This conversation is getting a bit heavy, and my coffee mug is empty. And, I really must be getting back home."

Angel took that as it was meant to be and rose. "Thank you, Bill, for the coffee, but mostly for the company. We'll be in touch, okay?"

"Good enough." He walked her to her car but didn't give her a goodbye hug. He was feeling uneasy, wondering where all this was going.

****

December came in with a vengeance. Snow and blowing snow covered the Valley. Angel stood with a cup of tea and looked out the front windows. She stared down the lane, and through tear-filled eyes she remembered how many times when she and Jake had first got married, that she had stood on that very spot and watched for him to come home, especially when there was a snow storm. But today Jake would not be coming home. It hit her hard.

Fortunately the school bus drove up at that time and Mae got out. She watched her daughter walk up the lane, pushing against the wind and the snow. Nothing on her head again…that child. But she would not scold her. She was taking things easy with Mae, after realizing that she must have felt threatened when Bill had been invited to dinner.

Mae popped the door open and rushed in with snow on her boots. "Stop right there, young lady. You look like a snowman and you weren't even out there long."

Mae's cheeks were rosy and she smiled at her mom. "It's snowing, Mom. I wish I could take the snowmobile out."

"Mae. You can't drive that thing alone. Your father always…" Angle changed the subject. "Wait until Rachael comes home. Maybe you two can go for a ride then."

Mae loved the snow and Angel recalled the many times when Jake would take his daughters riding with him. He would go out to the back of the house and into the woods and follow a path that took him directly to the manor. It was a long road and many snowmobilers used it.

Mae pushed off her jacket and kicked off her boots, wearing a scowl. "It won't be any fun this winter, if you won't let me take the snowmobile out."

"Mae, you're too young and that's the end of it."

Mae grabbed up her backpack and went upstairs, probably to sulk in her room, Angel thought.

The second Saturday in December brought more snow. Angel was looking forward to Rachael coming home and wondering if she should invite Tanya and Bob for Christmas dinner as she had every year. Since the meeting in the coffee shop, Angel hadn't seen or heard from Tanya. But that wasn't really unusual considering what Tanya was dealing with now. She decided to give her a call.

But Bob was the one who answered the phone. "Hi, Bob, it's Angel. How are you?" She wished she hadn't said that, even though it was a normal greeting for most people.

"I'm about the same," Bob replied, leaving Angel to wonder whether she should ask how that was or move on. She decided to move on.

"Is Tanya at home?"

"She is, but she's upstairs. Just a minute, I'll give her a call." Angel could hear Bob yelling to Tanya that it was Angel on the phone.

"She'll be right here."

"I hope I didn't drag her away from something important."

"Hey, a phone call from you, Angel is always important." Bob laughed in his cheerful way.

"I was just wondering if you two were coming for Christmas dinner this year."

"Well, don't we always? Unless of course you find it a bit too much this year. But then family should stick together, eh?"

"That's right, Bob." Angel had just finished her sentence when Tanya apparently had taken the phone.

"What's right?" she asked.

"Bob was just saying that family should stick together. I had been asking him—"

"Well, that's the way it used to be," Tanya replied in a terse tone.

"It still is, isn't it?" Angel was taken aback somewhat by Tanya's quick words.

"If you say so."

Angel decided to ignore that comment and move on to what she had called about. "Are you and Bob coming for Christmas dinner this year?"

"Well, don't we always? That is unless you have different plans this year. I wouldn't want to be a bother."

Angel had had enough. "Tanya, what in the world is wrong with you? You're not still upset over seeing me with Bill at the coffee shop are you?"

"I'm not upset."

"So, are you coming or not? I know you come every year, but I just wanted to check and make sure it wouldn't be an inconvenience in taking Bob out in the snow this year. We've had so much snow already."

"It's not a problem, Angel. I can't even imagine why you would think it would be. Bob might use the wheelchair, but you know he can still get around without it when he needs to."

Angel was having a hard time controlling her temper. She took a deep breath and waited, deciding not to comment further on that statement.

After a moment of silence, Tanya continued, "Shall I bring my normal pumpkin pies and cranberry sauce? I can do more, if you need me to."

"Of course, that's fine, Tanya. I'll be in touch. And don't worry, the girls are here to help out. It will be a small gathering this year."

She wished she had left that last part off, her mouth was always getting her in trouble lately, but Tanya didn't comment so Angel made a hasty exit from the phone.

"Well," she said out loud. "That went well...I think."

"What went well?"

Angel bobbed her head around to see Mae standing at the foot of the stairs. "Oh. I was just talking to your aunt about Christmas dinner."

"He's not coming, is he?"

"Who? Uncle Bob? Of course he—"

"No. That man."

Angel shook her head in frustration. "Mae, that man has a name, if you're talking about Mr. Canton."

"That's not what you call him."

"No. I call him, Bill, which is his name. And no, he's not coming."

"Good." Mae went into the kitchen and got juice from the refrigerator.

Angel decided to not continue the conversation. Sometimes the less said is the best. She thought of her Aunt May, who would have said, the least said the soonest mended. Her beloved aunt had many expressions and always brought them up at the appropriate time. How she missed her. If only she were here, Angel knew she would have some sound advice for all of this.

There would be two empty places at the Christmas table this year, and it was going to be a hard Christmas to get through. Jake had always loved Christmas, and Angel was determined to carry on and try and get through it as festively as she could manage.

****

It was a happy day for Angel when Rachael got home. Rachael always had a way of keeping things going. It was a part of her she had inherited from her dad. Mae had been spending the afternoon at a friend's house and Angel was anxiously waiting for Rachael to arrive. She was watching out the living room window when she spied Rachael's car coming up the driveway. Angel flung open the door and ran outside to greet her daughter.

"Oh, Mom. It's so great to be finally home for longer than a weekend." After they got Rachael's luggage out of the car and into the foyer, Rachael had questions. "So, how are things going, Mom? How's Mae. Is she doing okay?"

Angel decided she needed to talk to Rachael about a few things, and this was the perfect time, while they were alone. She and Rachael went into the living room and sat down.

"I'm a bit confused about how things are going right now, Rachael. I thought things were pretty good, but now I have to wonder, especially about your aunt."

"Aunt Tanya? What's going on with her?"

"Bob isn't doing so well. He's getting worse I guess. Tanya never elaborated but she's upset over it. And to make matters worse, I kind of stirred up a hornet's next…with her, and with Mae."

Rachael's eyes were large and questioning as Angel glanced over at her. "You? What did you do, Mom?"

"Well, I didn't think I did anything out of the way, but to hear Tanya talk—"

"Mom, you've got me curious. Start at the beginning, please."

"Before I go into that story, I have to tell you something else. I'm not going to sell the manor. I'm keeping it and turning it into a retreat."

"What?" Rachael's eyes were nearly popping out of her head by now.

"I just can't part with it. And I think it's going to make a great project for this area."

"Mom, you lost me."

Angel went on to tell Rachael the whole story of when she decided to convert the manor into a retreat for writers and artists. She told her about seeing Bill Canton and how he helped her with business decisions. She also told her about Mae's reaction when she invited Bill to dinner.

"I was surprised when Mae went straight to Tanya and told her about Bill coming for dinner. That's when Tanya got upset."

Rachael looked confused. "What was Aunt Tanya upset about?"

"She didn't think it was proper for me to have invited Bill to dinner."

"Mom, how well do you know this Bill Canton?"

"He and I have spent quite a bit of time together. Believe me, it's mostly business. However, I did visit him one day to go over some papers and he and I had lunch…then we went fishing."

"Fishing!"

"That's right, and it was fun. It was relaxing and there was no harm in it."

Rachael sat quietly, waiting for the next part, but Angel was done. She now waited for Rachael's reaction, but Rachael continued to just sit and stare at her.

"Well, say something, Rachael. Either get mad at me like Tanya and Mae or—"

"I'm not mad, Mom. I'm stunned. Wow. How come no one wrote me about all this stuff?"

"As far as I was concerned, Rachael, there was nothing really to write about except to tell you about the manor, and I asked Mae not to tell you because I wanted to do it in person when you got home."

"I see. And what's going on with you and Mr. Canton?"

Rachael's blue eyes were looking at her mother for an explanation better than the one she gave her before. Angel raised her voice. "Nothing's going on. He's advising me on builders and plumbers and electricians and landscapers, and—"

"Okay, Mom, I get the picture. Obviously, the others don't."

Angel calmed down. "That's right. So now you know what's been going on."

"Well." Rachael shook her head in astonishment. "This here retreat idea sounds big. Tell me more about it."

Angel got excited seeing at last that Rachael was not going to blast her about it, like the others had. Rachael always did have a more even temperament than Mae. She told Rachael all that she knew so far.

"Sounds exciting, and just what you probably need right now. You know I'm really glad that Aunt Tanya and Uncle Bob helped talk me into going back to college. I would have sat around and wasted my whole fall, or maybe a whole year."

"Yes, that's what I'm thinking. I need this project to get me back to the land of the living. It's not been easy living life without your father around."

Rachael gave Angel one of her compelling smiles. "I'm happy for you, Mom. If this is what you want to do. I'm excited for you too. Have you started renovating yet?"

"No, not yet. In the new year. I wanted to get Christmas over first. It's going to be a tough one."

"It sure is," Rachael muttered.

Angel looked over to see tears in Rachael's eyes. They fell into a quiet time. A lot had been said and Angel was relieved to at least have one family member on her side.

****

Tanya drove up and had Mae with her. Mae barely got in the door before she was asking for Rachael who had gone upstairs to unpack.

"Look who I found on her way home," Tanya said to Angel.

"Hey, Mae, I've got something for you, it's the coolest thing," Rachael called down the stairs. Mae took off upstairs to see what her big sister had brought her.

Tanya looked embarrassed as she stood facing Angel. Angel took Tanya's coat and hung it in the closet. She noticed Tanya's distressed look but was waiting for Tanya to make the first move.

When Angel went into the kitchen, Tanya followed. "You have every right not to speak to me, Angel. I'm sorry about the other day. I was really, really exhausted and out of line."

Angel took a roast from the fridge and gathered up seasonings for it. "I understand it's not easy for you now, Tanya. But you have to understand that I have a life also. My husband is dead and I can't lie down and die too. I'm excited about the retreat, and Bill is a great help when I need someone to talk to. He's been in business for years, much like Jake."

"I understand that...I do, and I'm sorry. I embarrassed myself, and you're right, it's your life."

Angel popped the roast in the oven and took a seat at the counter. Tanya continued to stand. "Let's put it behind us," Angel said with a smile. "Life is tough and if I make decisions that I regret later, then so be it. I'll deal with them then."

"You're very brave, Angel, and strong. A lot of people would fold up after a tragedy like you've gone through."

"That's not true. Most people survive very well, after the initial horror and shock. This retreat is my way of moving on, of bringing something meaningful into my life."

Tanya smiled. "I'm glad and I hope it works out. I also hope that William Canton will be a help. Lord knows he needs to redeem himself after what has happened."

"Tanya, you're wrong. Bill did nothing to cause the accident. It was circumstances. Yeah, he's dealing with some guilt, but it's not justified. I have to say at first I also felt resentful that he was alive and Jake was not, but I'm over that. I can't punish another person for what fate has thrown my way."

Tanya walked out of the kitchen. "Tell Rachael I expect her to come visit me tomorrow. Now that school's out, she can bring Mae."

Angel caught up with Tanya. She opened the closet door to retrieve Tanya's coat, then turned and hugged her sister-in-law. "We need to stay close, Tanya. Jake would want it that way. You and Jake's parents are Rachael's closest living relatives, next to Mae. And Rachael is happy for my decisions on the manor. Please be happy for me also."

Tanya hugged her back, and Angel saw tears in her eyes. "I really must apologize to Mr. Canton sometime. I feel like such a fool."

"I'm sure he understands. He's been through a bit himself in this lifetime. Don't worry about it."

After Tanya left, Angel got on the phone to Bill. She didn't plan to call him, but suddenly she wanted to talk to him. There was something about the sound of his voice that calmed her. And right now she needed that. It wasn't easy dealing with Jake's sister and the girls. They were all missing Jake terribly, but no one missed Jake like she did. Keeping herself together day after day was torture. One wrong turn or disagreement might set her back to the early fall days of such deep and torturing misery, that she felt she might never recover. Hang on, she told herself.

The panic receded when she heard his voice.

CHAPTER TEN

Mae had offered to set the table, but when Angel walked into the dining room, she stopped short. Everything was as normal. Places for Tanya and Bob, herself at the head, a place for Mae and Rachael, and also one for Aunt May and at the end of the table, a spot for Jake. It looked just like last year.

They had gotten through the holidays with some sad moments, some good times, some laughter and many tears. They talked about the past and Rachael talked about her future. Angel didn't mention the retreat. They shared old photos and memories. The opening of the gifts was a tough time. There was nothing from Jake, there was nothing for Jake, or Aunt May. Angel found it fitting to have a place at the table for them.

As they gathered around the table, they lifted their glasses in a toast, first to Jake, then to Aunt May. It was part sombre and part healing. Later talk turned to everyday things.

Angel was relieved when the day was done. She walked into the living room with a tea and sat on the sofa looking out at the covered pool. The pool lights were on and she watched them sparkle in the snow. Tanya and Bob had gone home, and the girls had retired to the upstairs. Angel waited for her visitor.

She jumped when the doorbell rang and hurried to it. Opening the door wide she greeted him. Bill Canton stood on the step with a paper wrapped package that he passed to Angel.

After entering the foyer and removing his winter gear, he explained, "I've been ice fishing."

"Oh, Bill, is it rainbow?"

"That it is, all cleaned and totally frozen."

She laughed. "That's a good thing considering that we'll be eating turkey for days. It'll be a welcome change later. Thank you." He hugged her in his usual way and she invited him into the living room. "I was just having tea, would you like a cup, or maybe wine?"

"No, I'm fine, thanks. I was really surprised to hear from you the other day. I figured you'd be busy with your family over the holidays." Bill sat on the sofa but not too close to Angel.

"Yes, we've been busy, mostly reminiscing." For a second her face took on a doleful expression, but changed to a smile as she looked back at him. "So what have you been up to? Did you visit family today?"

"No. I never do. Mom has Eric, that's all she needs. I spent the afternoon fishing. It was beautiful out on the lake today. Things are frozen up so early this year."

Angel sipped her tea but remained quiet. When they didn't talk about business or fishing she felt a bit awkward around him. She had brought up his family but he had dismissed them. Bill didn't let the silence last too long.

"So, Angel, why did you ask me here tonight?"

Angel was caught, not knowing what to answer she grew flustered. There was really no good reason she had invited him except that she wanted to see him. She thought fast. "Oh, I thought it would be nice if you met Rachael. I know you had a short chat with her at the cemetery, and she told me that she called you when you were in the hospital, but it would be nice if you met her again on better terms."

"Splendid."

Angel rose, glad to be out of that predicament, and walked to the stairs. "Girls, will you come down here, please?"

"In a minute," Rachael called.

"Bill, are you sure I can't get you something...a coffee maybe."

"Sure, that would be fine."

As Angel was returning to the living room, cup in hand, the girls came tumbling down the stairs. Mae had lightened up a lot since Rachael had come home. She almost seemed back to her old bubbly self, that is until she saw Bill in the living room.

Mae stopped in her tracks, while Rachael continued into the living room. Rachael started talking to Bill and sat on an opposite chair to the sofa.

"Mae," Angel said, "Come in, dear, just for a few minutes."

Mae followed her mother and Angel handed the coffee to Bill. Mae took a seat as far from Bill as she could find. She had already reverted back into her shell.

"So, you're in pre-vet studies at the ag college?"

"Second year," Rachael replied to Bill.

"I guess you're liking it?"

"I love it. It's what I've always wanted to do."

"It's nice to have a goal in life," Bill replied, sounding wistful.

Angel felt it was time to intervene. "I guess you two need no introduction. I just wanted you girls to know," she looked at Rachael then over at Mae, "that Bill is going to be hanging around here sometimes. He's helping me figure out how to put this retreat together. So what do you girls think of my idea anyway?"

"I told you, Mom, if it makes you happy, go for it," Rachael said.

Angel looked at Mae. "And what do you think, darling? I'm hoping to call on your artistic ability for some ideas—"

"I think it's the dumbest idea I've ever heard of, and I don't want any part of it. Can I go now?"

"Mae, don't be rude."

Mae jumped up and ran to her mother, throwing her arms around her and wailing her heart out. "Oh, my goodness, Mae, what in the world—"

"I think I should leave." Bill rose.

"No," Angel said sharply.

Rachael jumped up and grabbed Mae. "We'll go upstairs, Mom. I'll talk to her."

Angel wrung her hands, and Bill moved closer. He touched her arm. "Look, if I caused this, I'm sorry, and I really should go."

Angel turned her face to his. "No, Bill. You did nothing wrong. Mae's just a child and I guess she feels threatened by you, or something."

"She definitely doesn't like me."

"It's not you. It's what you represent. She misses her father."

"All the more reason for me *not* to be here, especially now during the holidays. It must be damn tough."

Tears glistened in Angel's eyes. "You don't know how tough. And that's why you need to stay. Rachael will talk to Mae and I will, tomorrow or later tonight. But right now, don't go. When things went wrong there was always Jake. He and I would work stuff out together. Now there's just me."

"Angel, I can't fill in for Jake."

"I'm not asking you to."

"Yes, you are."

"Am I?"

"Look, I know you're lonely, you miss him, I get that. I'm lonely too. I had a wife once, I thought the world of her, but things went bad and she wanted a life away from me. I never figured out if it was something I did, something I said, or just that she was tired of me. It hurts like hell. But not half as much as it must hurt, when you lose someone you love, to death…someone who never intended to leave you."

Angel stared at him, tears running down her cheeks. He held her hand but stayed a distance from her. He did not know what was expected of him. He thought it was the Christmas season, the memories that she did not want to go away. She was clinging to him and he was confused. He noticed a tissue box on the mantel and went for it. He passed one to Angel and remained standing.

"I have to go. It's not the right time for me to be here. I know you want to talk and I want to listen. Jake was a friend of mine, he was a great guy. We can have those conversations, after the holidays. Please, Angel, spend this time with your girls, they need you, even ever-so-brave, Rachael. She's just a kid yet herself, and she's trying to be a mother to Mae. Be strong, Angel, go to your girls. I'll catch up with you after the holidays, okay?"

****

After Bill left, Angel knew he was right, and it was not the time for her to have invited him to the house. He was a wise man, and he seemed genuinely concerned, not only for her, but for her girls as well.

She walked upstairs and found Rachael in Mae's room. Rachael was listening to music and reading, while Mae was at her usual post, drawing. Angel stood in the doorway and Rachael removed her ear phones. "I'm sorry, girls. I was wrong to ask Bill here tonight. He's gone now. I'm sorry, Mae. I know you don't like him. And Rachael, this time while you're home, should be our time, yours, mine and Mae's. How about we go out and see how the snowmobile looks tomorrow. If the weather is right, maybe you could take Mae for a ride, Rachael."

Mae finally looked up from her drawing. Her face lit up and she even grew a smile. "Really?"

"Let's do it," Rachael agreed, while plugging her ear phones back in.

Angel left the girls to what they were doing before and went back downstairs. She was slightly embarrassed over the evening's events. What had come over her? Why had she broken down in front of Bill that way? She was not as strong as she had thought she was, but he knew it, and he understood.

****

The sun was blinding on Boxing Day, when Angel and the girls headed out to the garage to have a look at the snowmobile.

"Things are quite the mess out here right now," Angel remarked. "Jake was going to clean it up before winter set in. I'm sorry."

"What, Mom? Sorry for what?"

"For mentioning your dad."

Rachael turned and walked back to her mom. "Why would you be sorry? Dad might not be here but he was once and we can talk about him, right Mae?"

Mae nodded.

"I know you're right, girls. I just didn't want to put a damper on the day."

"What? By talking about Dad? He'll always be our dad and he'll always be in our lives," Rachael said.

Angel moved on. "Remember, this is the new machine. Your dad hardly got to use it. He was looking forward to all of us going out together this winter."

"Where's the old snowmobile?" Mae asked.

"It's at the manor. There just wasn't room here for both of them."

Rachael reached the snowmobile and pulled the tarp off it. Mae ran over and helped her. "Wow, it's a beautiful machine. But I don't know if I can drive this one."

"Maybe we should go over to the manor then and you can use the old one."

They all piled in Angel's car and drove to the manor. Angel had hired someone to plough out the property driveway for the winter. "You girls can go out to the shed. I'm going in and have a look around inside, make sure there's no damage going on. If you need my help, come get me."

Angel entered the hallway. The house smelled musty, and Angel shivered. It looked so forlorn. She remembered the cold winter days when she would visit and Aunt Mae would always have a fire humming and a cup of tea for her. Angel wiped a tear from the corner of her eye.

It wasn't long before she heard the snowmobile motor. She went to the living room window and saw the girls taking off up the back lane. She had told them to be back in at least an hour. Angel climbed the stairs and looked around. Everything seemed to be okay, but the house was still full of furniture. She would have to do something about that. She decided to run an ad in the paper or list some items online.

She walked downstairs to the kitchen to find a notepad. May always kept a few in the top drawer by the sink. There they were, three of them and pens and pencils in the drawer as well. Angel grabbed one and a pen and proceeded back upstairs. She had decided to make a list of the furniture items she would be selling.

The snowmobile whined into the yard and before long the girls were clamouring into the house saying they were freezing. Angel was slightly cold herself\and was glad to get in the car and on their way back home.

The rest of the holiday break went by swiftly and it was soon time for Rachael to pack her car up and leave.

"Gonna miss you guys," Rachael said through tear-filled eyes.

After final hugs all around Rachael hurried to the car, and Angel and Mae were left standing on the front veranda harbouring their tears.

****

It was mid January when Angel finally met with the construction owner. She decided to do it on her own, feeling that if she called Bill it might make her look too dependent, and she certainly didn't want to appear as a lonely widow needing a back-up.

Ever since the Christmas night visit from Bill, Angel had been embarrassed by what had taken place. She certainly didn't want to put him in the middle of any place that he might not want to be.

She felt a bit discouraged after the meeting. There was so much to do, so much to decide. She sat in front of the fireplace, papers spread out around her, not knowing where to start. Frustration was getting the best of her. She decided to pour a glass of wine to relax a bit. She was in the kitchen pouring a drink, when the doorbell rang.

A surprised Angel opened the door to see Bill Canton standing before her. He smiled. "Hi," he said.

"Bill. What a surprise. Please come in."

Bill removed his coat and Angel took it. He slipped off his boots and commented, "That wine looks good."

Angel smiled. "I'll get you a glass." She left for the kitchen.

Bill made himself comfortable on the living room sofa. He saw the mess of papers on the floor surrounding one of the big armchairs. Angel entered the room holding a glass of wine towards him.

"Thanks. Looks like you're busy."

"I was, but it's all so confusing."

"What's got you confused?"

"Everything. I don't know where to start."

"Good thing I dropped by then." He placed his wine glass on a table and walked over to retrieve the papers, carrying them back to where he had been sitting. "Everything looks in order with this estimate. I'd say it's a pretty good one."

"Yes, probably, but maybe because I haven't a clue what I was supposed to include."

"Then you should have waited."

I can't wait forever," Angel spoke sharply.

"Well, I've got something that might lift your spirits." Bill took a memory stick from his pocket. "Got a computer?"

Angel walked over to the book shelves and retrieved a laptop. She passed it to Bill and he turned it on. "What do you have?"

Bill inserted the stick and motioned Angel to sit down. Angel took a seat on the sofa beside him and watched as he pulled up a website.

"Wow," she exclaimed. "Is that my retreat?" She looked at the screen which displayed Angel's Retreat at the top. "It's the manor."

"Yep. I went over and took a picture of it."

"How did you know where it was?"

"Found some old info online of when it was a B and B."

"Oh, playing detective. It's so pretty, isn't it?"

"It's going to look great, Angel. As you can see I don't have much on here, but the general set up. This is your homepage, and this website is going to be one of your main promotional tools.

"Here we have your type of retreat, Writers and Artists, with separate pages at the top to click to. This will determine your audience and activities. If you can think of something, like maybe a theme, that would be great. People love anything that is theme based. For example, you might want to create theme rooms, or an overall theme."

"I never thought of that."

"Your website will highlight all the benefits your retreat has to offer. This will be your amenities page, where you can describe what your retreat is like and what you have to offer. You might want to stick with a country manor theme. I like that idea."

"I do too," Angel agreed.

"Down the line you might want to find speakers for your events. This will be your events page. Your home page will give your basic info, ie the picture, the location, and all that stuff. Then there's your contact page where you will put the address, and other contact info. A lot of websites around here use a long photo of the Bay of Fundy. It's something to consider, and that could be used as an intro page as well."

"There's so much to consider."

"I've found quite a few links that I've listed below. Take a look at some of them to get ideas. Your best bet to help you form your vision is the Internet. You'll probably find that you come up with some of your own ideas after looking at others. That's what I did, but my website is not nearly as detailed as yours will have to be. You are complicating matters as well by having artists and writers."

"I don't think that will be a complication. Wow, this thing will be so big, so much to consider."

"Anyway, there should be lots of rooms since you won't be living there."

"Oh, but I will."

Bill looked surprised. "You will? But, what about this house?"

"I'm planning to sell it."

"Oh. Well, in that case, you might want to consider remodelling the top floor into a suite for the family. Of course you won't need a kitchen, you can use the main one."

"That's an idea. I don't know where I thought we were going to stay. You can see I haven't given much thought to this whole thing, up until now."

"Well, you've got your work cut out for you, I'd say, and plenty of it."

Angel threw her arms around Bill. "I can't thank you enough. This does look daunting right now, but without your help to get started, I was lost."

Bill responded to Angel's hug with one of his own, and in the gleeful moment, he kissed her.

Angel pulled back, startled, and he apologized. "God, Angel, I'm sorry. I got lost in the moment."

But Angel smiled back at him. "Guess we both were lost there…for a minute."

Bill snapped the laptop shut and got up. He didn't know what else to do. He was feeling weird about kissing Angel, even though she never made a big deal of it. Why did he do it? But, it just felt so natural.

"I'll leave the stick with you. I have a copy. If there's anything you think of you want to add, just give me a call. We can work together that way."

"Okay, that sounds great. My first priority, I think, would be to envision what the manor should look like, then I can give Mr. Barre a better idea for when he can get started."

"Good idea. I'm glad I inspired you."

Angel rose and took the laptop from Bill, returning it to the bookcase shelf. She walked back to face him. "You do inspire me, Bill. Before you came tonight, I was doubting myself and the whole venture. It just seemed so big and I didn't know where to start."

"You should have called me."

"I…I thought I shouldn't."

Bill got up and stood before her. "Why's that, Angel?"

Angel dropped her eyes and stared at the floor. "Well, ever since Christmas I've been feeling a bit embarrassed about when you were here."

Bill put an arm behind Angel's back and guided her back to the sofa. He looked into her eyes. "I thought as much, that's why I waited a while before coming over. Of course it took me some time also to get this thing put together." Angel was quiet and he felt an awkwardness between them. "Are you upset with me?"

"No. Why should I be?"

"For kissing you. It was impulsive of me and I'm sorry. It's just been a long time."

"You don't date?"

"Kinda hard to trust again."

"Yep, I know the feeling."

"You trusted Jake?"

"Of course, I'm not talking about Jake. My first husband, James."

"Oh, yeah, you did mention an ex."

"It was a long time ago, but I remember it well. It was hard for me to trust…until I met Jake, and the poor man, he must have been a saint because he never gave up on me."

"I'm sorry you had a hard time with your ex. Did he cheat on you?"

"No, that wasn't it. I mean, I don't think he did, he could have, but that wasn't the issue. He was abusive…verbally and emotionally. I was a mess. It took me a long time to gain any self confidence, but Jake was always there for me, always one step ahead." A tear slid down Angel's cheek. and she reached up and brushed it aside with the back of her hand.

Bill put his arms around her then he pulled back. "Where's Mae?"

"Oh, Mae's in bed of course."

"I...I just wouldn't want her to get any wrong ideas."

"Like what, Bill?"

"Ah...me hugging you."

"And, you kissing me?"

He nodded.

Angel walked to the patio doors and stood looking out. "Since we're baring our souls tonight, what about your wife? Did she cheat on you?"

"Big time, and with my best friend."

"That sucks."

"Big time."

"Any kids?"

"Nope, lucky that way."

"Yeah, kids in the middle always get the worst of the deal. I've seen many of them in my classes."

"Were you a teacher?"

"I used to be." She walked back towards the sofa, but kept going to the kitchen. When she came back she carried the wine bottle and refilled their glasses.

"You're quite the woman, Angel, a teacher turned artist."

"Turned mother, now business woman." She grinned.

"I hope this is going to work out for you. I'll do whatever I can to help, you know that."

"Bill, you've been amazing. For someone I just met, I feel like I've known you forever."

"I get the same feeling, almost as if somewhere back in time, we did."

"Now you're getting spooky."

Bill laughed and tipped up his wine glass. "Good wine."

"It should be, it's the same kind you brought for dinner."

He laughed again.

Angel was now sitting beside him. He reached over and touched her hand. "I like being with you, Angel. You're very comforting to talk to."

"Yeah, but do you trust me?"

"Yes, I do. Maybe I shouldn't but I really do. You have no idea how long it's been since I've shared anything with another person."

"What about your family?"

"My dad's out there somewhere. I think he's in British Columbia. He was always kind of a hippie, probably on some island somewhere, maybe a loner just like me."

"Are you like him?"

"Hah. Ask my mom. She thinks so. She never stopped telling me so all my life. I was no good like him...I had a temper like him."

"You...have a temper?"

He grinned. "I can have, if I'm pushed. And my wife knew how to push my buttons. But I tell you, it was never physical. I never laid a hand on her. Hell, I didn't even know she was sleeping around until she told me. That was just before she presented me with divorce papers."

She touched his hair and smoothed it back. "Poor Bill."

And he couldn't help himself again. This time he took her in his arms and kissed her more fervently, and she didn't pull away. She returned his kisses as passionately as he had given his. Long minutes were lost in deep kissing and caresses, until she finally pulled from him. She looked him in the eyes, put both hands on his face, tilted his chin towards her face and said, "That was beautiful, Bill, but where are we going to go with this?"

CHAPTER ELEVEN

Angel lay in bed thinking about the peculiar evening. She was surprised at herself. When Bill Canton had kissed her the first time, she barely thought anything of it. It was a moment of joy and he just got carried away.

But the second time was different, and still she wasn't shocked. She had kissed him back with just as much passion and desire as she felt from him. It was like something magical had happened, and all the past and thoughts of guilt or longing for Jake had just vanished into thin air. At that moment there was no Jake, no children, no pain and misery, there was just her and Bill.

It was an experience like she had never had before. She shivered when she recalled his earlier words. *I get the same feeling, almost as if somewhere back in time, we did.* And it was true she did feel like she'd known him forever, ever since their first meeting. Although she had gone there ready for a confrontation, she found she didn't get one from him. She was hurt and blamed him for Jake's death, but hearing Bill describe Jake's last moments to her was just a peaceful, comforting feeling.

Bill had left shortly after she had asked where they were going with everything. He just shrugged and said, "Guess we'll just have to go and find out." And they left it at that. No drama, no promises.

The guilt set in when Angel rose in the morning. She had tiptoed into Mae's room the night before and watched her daughter sleeping. Now she was on her way down to Mae's room again to wake her up for school.

She was surprised when she opened the door and Mae was already up. "Oh, you're an early bird. This is unusual. Usually I have to practically pull you out of bed."

Mae looked sullen. She was sitting at her desk brushing her hair. "Can you put these clips in for me?" she asked her mother. She handed them to Angel.

Angel had one in and was struggling with the other when Mae spoke up, "He was here last night, wasn't he?"

"What?"

"That man, Mr. Canton. I heard you guys talking downstairs. I couldn't make out much of what you said but I heard you laugh a couple of times, and he did too. What was he doing here, Mom?"

"Yes, Bill was here. He surprised me, I wasn't expecting him, but he's making a website for the manor for when I turn it into a retreat. You should see it, Mae, it's quite interesting looking. Maybe you'll have some ideas for me, to help me build it."

"I don't want to help, but Rachael said I shouldn't be rude to him anymore. She said it wasn't polite to be rude to someone's friends."

"Oh, did she?"

"Yes, she did."

"Well, I'm glad, Mae, because Mr. Canton likes you a lot. He thinks you're very smart and pretty."

"I won't be rude, but I don't have to like him, do I?"

Angel checked the time. Since Mae had been up and dressed early, they had a few minutes. She sat down on the bed and questioned her daughter. "Why don't you like him, Mae? Did he say something to you that hurt you?"

"No."

"Then how did he offend you?"

"He didn't offend me. I just don't like him."

"You have to have a reason, Mae. He's a very nice man, and Rachael likes him."

"Mom, I'm hungry, let's go downstairs."

Angel laid a hand on Mae's shoulder. "No. We're not going anywhere until you tell me the truth. You don't just dislike someone for no reason."

"I don't want him here. I don't want him in Daddy's house."

"Oh, Mae, I thought it was something like that. He's not trying to take your daddy's place. He was your dad's friend, yes, and now he's my friend, but that's it, he's just a friend. And he's helping me with business."

Mae turned and looked at Angel. "Are you sure?"

Angel laughed. "Yes, Mae, I've very sure. You can relax because Mr. Canton is not trying to be in your daddy's shoes. Why he would never think of a thing like that. In fact he doesn't even have children. He probably doesn't know anything about kids, like your dad did."

Angel tried to convince Mae in a simple way, hoping she was getting through to her. It was difficult to know with Mae because she kept her feelings so locked up most of the time.

"Can we have breakfast now, Mommy?"

Angel shrugged. "Sure, come on."

****

With Mae off to school, Angel was anxious to get her laptop and have another look at the website. She felt that if she could fill out some of the information about the retreat then she would have a better idea what to tell the workers when the time came.

Every day after that, she would sit and work as long as she could. One afternoon towards the end of January, the door bell rang. Angel's heart jumped. She hadn't heard from Bill since he'd been over about the website. She thought it was a bit odd, but she felt odd herself about calling him, after what had taken place that night.

She opened the door to tall, lanky Arnold Brooks. "Why, Arnold what a pleasant surprise!"

Angel took his coat and after Arnold had removed his footwear, she invited him into the living room. "Take a seat by the fire, you must be chilly."

"It's true, Angel, my old bones can't hold the heat like they used to. I'm older than May you know, I'm on my way to 92…just hopin' I make it." His laugh quickly turned into a frown. "Course, there's not many left that I knew in my younger days. All my old friends have gone away." He looked at Angel with misty eyes.

Angel quickly bent down and put her hand on his shoulder. "I'm so sorry, Arnold. I know how much a comfort May was to you after Mabel passed on. And now she's gone too. I miss her too, Arnold." She gave Arnold a hug, and he sniffed and hauled out his red hanky with the white dots. He must have had a dozen of them, Angel thought. "Would you like a cup of tea, Arnold?"

"That would be right dandy. Boy, that fire sure feels good though."

After Angel brought them both tea, Arnold was full of questions. "May's house is lookin' pretty dismal these days. And I don't even see a for sale sign on it. How come you haven't sold it, Angel?"

Angel smiled as she sat across from him. "Well, I've got big plans for the manor. In fact, before you came I was just working on a website." She saw that she'd lost Arnold, so she went on to explain. "I've decided to keep the property and turn it into a retreat."

Arnold looked confused.

"I want to turn the place into a beautiful retreat for writers and artists. A place where they can come and do their work, undisturbed. When they feel like it, they can roam outside, walk through the orchards and down by the stream."

Arnold got a dreamy look on his face. "It sounds heavenly. When are you doin' all this?"

"There's so much to do, and I'm a little apprehensive about the enormity of the whole thing, but I've got some help and that's why I'm working on the website. If I can create an informative website and dream up stuff to put on there, then I can follow through at the manor. I know it's kind of backwards, but it's my plan anyway."

Arnold sighed. "There's so much history there."

Angel got an idea. "Arnold, would you like to help me out? Maybe you could write up a history of the place, and I could have that for my website as well."

Arnold's face took on a glow. "Well, now, I could probably do just that. Might take some time—"

"I've got time."

"Okie dokie then." Arnold drained the bottom of his cup and rose. "I should be on my way. I want to get started on this history thing. And I think your retreat will be something. Yes, I can see the people comin' up the lane." Arnold stretched his long arm to its limit as he emphasized the string of guests arriving. He bent slightly and drew his face close to Angel's. "It will be a dandy affair," he whispered in her ear.

Angel laughed at his glee. It made her happy to have a visit from Arnold and for him to leave on a much happier note than when he had arrived. She also thought he would do a great job of putting together a history of the manor and the area surrounding it. Angel could see it framed, hanging in the hallway when guests arrived to read it.

After Arnold had departed she got back to the laptop and her imagination. She was thinking of theme rooms, and at the same time trying to picture what she wanted the inside of the manor to look like. She would go online and look at more retreats, and more websites to acquaint herself with how to add information to hers.

****

It was a Saturday, the last one in January. Mae was over visiting with Tanya and Bob, and Angel was alone again. She sat with her laptop and a steaming cup of coffee by her side, looking at the descriptions she had written up of her theme rooms. She had decided to go with the country manor theme. She had also decided to gut the kitchen and modernize it. The French doors that May had put in when she was running her bed and breakfast would be great, because it gave easy access to the dining area, a great convenience for guests.

Her plan now was also to have a kitchen installed on the upper floor for herself. The guests would be able to prepare their own food in the big kitchen downstairs. The top floor had never been open to guests during the bed and breakfast era. It was where Angel had her small bedroom and where Aunt May had a bedroom as well, even though she later moved to the bedroom on the first floor, the one she had occupied when Angel had first arrived at the manor so many years ago.

The old Victorian house had so much country charm. It sat on a hill overlooking the mighty tides of the Bay of Fundy. The antique fireplace would be an ideal spot to curl up with a book from the built-in bookcase. As Angel thought of the manor it gave her fodder to work with. She got busy describing the bedrooms, the living room, and even imagining what the new updated kitchen would look like. She was having fun for the first time since…since Jake, she thought. Life was divided now. There was her life with Jake and now her life after Jake. Angel wished that Bill would call or something. It had been a long time since she'd heard from him, and she wondered why. But still she was reluctant to call him.

Before Angel was to pick up Mae, she stopped in for a few groceries. She was rounding a corner and bumped a cart, only to look up into Bill Canton's face. "Oh," she said in surprise. "Sorry, I was deep in thought."

Bill grinned slightly. "Thinking about that retreat, I bet."

"Well, yes, I've been very busy with the website. You'd be surprised at what I've done."

"I'm glad." Bill moved his cart aside to let Angel into the aisle.

She parked it to one side and asked, "Where have you been, Bill?"

He gave her that lopsided grin again and replied, "I'm been home, I guess."

"Bill, what's wrong? You're acting weird."

"No, I'm not."

"Yes, you are. I haven't heard a thing from you in weeks."

"Really, Angel, it's no big deal. It looks like you've been keeping busy."

"Well, yeah, but it would be nice to have someone to run these things by, just for a second opinion, you know?"

"Then send me the website and I'll look it over."

Angel was at a loss for words, but she didn't really have to worry about that because Bill wasn't.

"I don't think this is the place to get into a deep conversation."

"Probably not," Angel replied.

"Send me the website and I'll get back to you with my opinion."

"No. You don't have to. I can see I've taken up way too much of your time." Angel moved on, giving her cart a giant push forward. When she reached the end of the aisle, she turned and glanced around briefly, but Bill was no where to be seen.

Angel finished up her shopping and got in the car. As she drove towards Tanya's house, she was flabbergasted. What in the world had gotten into him anyway? Maybe this was his personality. Maybe he was bipolar or something. Maybe that was why his wife left him, and he didn't get along with his family. Could explain a lot, and if so, it was something she didn't need in her life. She had enough to deal with now.

Angel drove in with the intention of going inside, but Mae was waiting and ran out to the car and hopped in. She was in a good mood as she told Angel what fun she had with her Aunt Tanya and Uncle Bob, and how they'd played board games and cards all afternoon.

Angel smiled, happy to see her daughter in a cheerful mood. "I think we should have Arnold Brooks over sometime. He loves to play cards and games."

"But Mommy, he's a hundred years old."

Angel laughed. "Not quite, but you're close." Angel drove through

Apple Grove, back past the grocery store and wondered if Bill was still in town. It had put a big damper on her day, and although she had not wanted to admit it, it had put a damper on her life as well.

****

Angel wasted no time feeling sorry for herself. If Jake were around, he wouldn't let something get in the way of one of his business deals. She had a project and she had to move forward, it was really all that was keeping her going, besides her kids of course.

Angel made a call to Barre Construction to see when they might get started. She had a more defining plan in her head now. When the owner hummed and hawed, seemingly putting her off a bit, Angel stood strong.

"You can't be this busy in the middle of winter, can you? This is going to be a big project and if you can't take it on, let me know so I can try and find someone else."

The mention of her backing out, struck a chord with the owner. "Hey, I didn't say anything about not taking it on. I suppose I could get started in a week or so."

"Good. Then I will meet with you someday this coming week. I'd like you to come by my house, as I have some definite ideas and plans and pictures that I would like to run by you."

She hung up the phone feeling victorious. In the future she had to be more assertive. She was alone now, a woman who had to take charge if she wanted to get things done. But oh, how she wished she could hop in the car and go over and talk to her Aunt May. For years now Angel had been running things by her aunt. And May, God love her soul, always had words of wisdom.

From that day forward, when Angel would run up on a problem, she would stop, take some time and think, what would May do or say in this situation?

By the middle of February, Angel was standing in the manor hallway, in the centre of one giant mess. There were workers coming and going in all directions, asking her questions, telling her stuff, solving problems, making problems, and any number of other probable chaotic situations going on.

She was on the phone talking to an auction house, when she turned around to see Bill Canton standing by the doorway. Angel almost dropped her phone; in fact she flipped it off in the middle of the conversation and shoved it in her pocket. "What are you doing here?"

Bill grinned, and had to speak up over the noise. "I was just driving by and noticed all the vehicles, so I thought I'd stop in and see how things were going."

"Oh, nice of you." Angel knew she was sounding sarcastic, but that's the way she felt. Was he now in his other mood and thinking she would just forget the other day?

"Can we talk, maybe somewhere quieter?"

Angel gave him a look, studied him for a minute, then moved towards the stairs. "I guess it will have to be upstairs. I've got people gutting the third floor as well, but the second floor is pretty calm right yet." She led Bill up to one of the old bed and breakfast rooms. After he entered she closed the door. "Well, talk."

He looked at her guiltily. "Look, I'm sorry about the other day. But you have to understand that when I left your house the last time, I thought I was going crazy."

"What?"

Bill had been circling the room but finally found a chair and perched himself on it. He ran his hand across the top of his head. "I mean, we were just sitting there talking and all of a sudden we were kissing. And neither of us wanted to stop. At least I don't think so." He looked up at her, but Angel, still standing in the centre of the room, said nothing. "Well, I know I didn't. And I know it was crazy, but you didn't tell me to stop. You didn't seem upset, I mean, what in thee hell was going on?"

"So we had a kiss. Is that reason enough to be rude to me the other day? Are you bi polar or something?"

Bill laughed slightly. "No, Angel. I'm not. If I was maybe that would help explain things, right?"

"Well, yes."

"I just went home and I thought and I thought and I thought. But I couldn't still figure out how we did what we did in such a casual yet almost passionate way, then just say goodnight and that was it."

"I was waiting to hear from you."

"I'm sorry. I got cold feet. I felt like hell. I felt so guilty and like such a creep. I mean, Jake was a friend of mine." He looked up at Angel again. "Can you explain how you felt that night? Because if you can, maybe it will help me to understand what the hell is going on."

Angel walked over and sat on the foot of the bed. She paused for a moment, then looked him in the eye. "It was sort of a strange thing. But I went to bed, feeling like it was normal. It felt normal to me. I didn't feel like I did anything wrong, even though I agree with you, how could we do that to Jake? Then come morning I got feeling guilty. But I had a chat with Mae, who by the way is not going to be rude to you anymore. She says that Rachael told her it was rude of her to be rude to someone's friends. That was enough I guess to convince Mae. But, I have to tell you, she said she doesn't like you, and it's because she doesn't want you in her daddy's house."

"See. Even a child knows better than we do. It wasn't right."

"But it felt right."

"It did. It felt natural and normal, as if we did it all the time."

"So you decided to start avoiding me and in that way avoiding the issue?"

"I did. I'm a coward. But I'm here now. After we met in the store, I couldn't stop thinking about how I'd treated you. I had to come and at least let you know why I did it and how I'm feeling." He got up and walked over to her. "Angel, I don't know what's going to happen, but I don't want to dance on my friend's grave."

Angel looked into his eyes. "I think I understand now. It's not me you're rejecting, but you're feeling guilty."

"I feel like a shit."

Angel took his hands. "Bill, you gotta understand something. If Jake were alive and we were kissing somewhere, then you should feel like a shit, and I should too. But Jake is not alive. If he were, none of this situation would have even taken place. I probably would not even know you. I think you're mixing your personal feelings up with what your wife did to you, with your best friend. Now that was different. Those two are two shits, and they deserve each other."

Bill grinned. "I have to agree."

"You and I, on the other hand, were put into a situation that brought us together. We liked each other and we enjoyed each other's company. You were helpful to me as well, and I leaned on you in that way. You were more than happy to offer me your assistance, maybe out of guilt, maybe not, but that was what happened. We found an attraction and we kissed. How can that be wrong? It's like saying that Jake should never have married me because his wife, Rosaline died. Should he have forever clung to her memories and brought Rachael up on his own?"

"But that's different. Jake's wife was dead, what two years?"

"Yes, it's different in some people's eyes. But we don't have to act on this, only if we want to. We can just go along and see what comes of it. If our feelings grow stronger towards each other, why should it be anyone else's business? I know that's what my Aunt May would say. Don't stick your nose into someone else's business."

"That may be true enough, but it is your girls' business, and it's also Jake's sister's business."

"No, it's not. I will deal with my girls. And Tanya will be fine. If she's not, then she will just have to learn to deal with it."

Bill grinned. "I didn't know you were so hard-nosed."

"I'm not, not really. But I might have to take a stand. I value your friendship, Bill, and I like you. I want you to be with me in this thing. I need you. I need your expertise. And God, I have to get back downstairs and see what everyone's doing. It seems they don't know what they're doing unless I'm around. And I tried to call an auction house, you know, when I saw you, I hung up on him." Angel looked shocked.

Bill laughed heartily. He reached down and gave Angel a hug and a pat on the back. "Don't worry, Angel. I know a great auctioneer. I'll give him a call and get his advice. You going to have an estate auction?"

"I have everything figured out that I want to let go, and I'd like to get it out of the house."

"I'll get on it. I guarantee I can have this stuff out of your way by tomorrow at the latest."

Angel rose. "Oh, Bill, it's such a relief to have my friend back. Talk to me, okay? Don't just go slinking off in a corner to lick your wounds, please?"

"I'll try."

They left the bedroom and went downstairs, where everyone was looking for Angel. While she was trying to answer workers' questions, Bill got on the phone to his auctioneer friend.

CHAPTER TWELVE

Angel was amazed to see what two weeks of work could do. Already the new kitchen in the manor was taking shape, and upstairs in her new apartment, the kitchen was already mostly in place. It would be a much smaller living area for Angel and the girls, but she did have the rest of the manor to look after as well, once everything was complete.

It was a lot easier to manoeuvre around in the manor, now that a lot of the unnecessary furniture that Angel had wanted disposed of was removed. The next day after Bill had shown up at the manor, a truck arrived to take it off to an auction recommended by Bill's auctioneer friend. It was a relief to Angel and she was glad that she and Bill had come to terms with the kisses. She hadn't wanted it to be a big deal; in fact she didn't even know what it meant. Was she developing feelings for Bill Canton or had both of them just been lonely?

Whatever it was, it hadn't happened again and each of them was far too busy to think about it. Well, at least she knew that she was, most of the time. But there were moments, when she was alone in bed at night drifting off to sleep, that the kiss would come back like a flash across her mind. It was almost like that feeling one gets, Angel thought, when you're drifting off to sleep and you don't know if you're asleep or awake.

It was the week before spring break and Angel was looking forward to Rachael coming home from NSAC. Then the phone call came. Rachael was not coming home. She told her mother that she had some heavy studying to do before midterm exams began. She also wanted to take a day and go to Wentworth for some skiing with some friends. Angel was disappointed but knew that Rachael had a life to live, and Rachael assured her mother that she would be home for Easter.

The last Saturday in February Angel was baking a cake, when she heard the sound of a snowmobile whining nearby. She paid little attention as it was not an unusual sound at that time of year in that area. But when the sound grew closer then stopped, she went to the window to have a look. Someone in snowmobile gear was leaning over the machine, and when he straightened and pulled off his helmet, she saw that it was Bill.

She opened the door and called, "What are you doing so far from home on that thing?"

He came up the walkway and said with a smile, "That thing can go almost anywhere this time of year."

Bill got his gear off in the hallway and by then Mae was at the foot of the stairs looking curiously at him. He looked up. "Hi, Mae, it's a great day for snowmobiling, do you like to ride?"

She grinned and nodded her head affirmatively, still keeping her distance.

Angel came from the kitchen holding a steaming, hot cup in her hand. "I just made a fresh pot of coffee, I'm sure it will hit the spot right about now."

"Oh, thanks." He made his way to the first chair in the living room and sat. The house smelled good, and that enticing aroma was coming from the kitchen. Bill's stomach rumbled.

Angel stood in front of him, her hands on her hips. "I just made a cake; it will be ready in a couple of minutes. You like hot cake?"

Bill's smile widened. "Do I have a mouth?"

Angel laughed. "You most definitely do."

Angel's remark took Bill back to the night he had kissed her. He hadn't forgotten what that was like and he was not apt to anytime soon.

Mae entered the living room and sat across from Bill. "What kind of snowmobile do you have?"

"It's an old one," Bill said. "A 2004 Ski Doo. I had hopes of upgrading a couple of years ago, but it didn't work out. Anyway, it still rides great. So I take it you like to ride?"

"I do, but I don't get to go. Rachael took me out at Christmas, but Mommy won't let me ride on my own. Daddy used to let me, around the fields where he could watch me, he said."

Bill had noticed that this was the most conversation he had ever gotten out of Mae. He decided to milk the subject further. "So, would you like to go for a ride, today?"

Mae's eyes lit up, but she didn't reply. She seemed undecided. "I don't know," she finally remarked. But when Angel came in the room with three plates of hot cake covered in ice cream, Mae was all over her. "Mommy, Mr. Canton asked me to go for a ride on his snowmobile. Is it okay?"

Angel looked surprised, but she continued into the room and placed the cake plates around. "Would you like more coffee, Bill?" Angel took his cup.

"Mommy."

"I heard you, Mae."

"Well?"

"I'll be right back." Angel made an exit to the kitchen.

Bill was not sure what was happening here, but he was soon to find out. Angel called to him from the kitchen.

Bill got up and hunched his shoulders towards Mae, who was staring at him.

Angel wasted no time once Bill reached the kitchen. Her voice remained low but he got the message. "Why did you ask my daughter to go snowmobiling, before you checked with me?"

Bill gulped. His shoulders went up again and his hands flew out in explanation. "It was a spur-of-the-moment thing. She just seemed like she really liked riding and I just asked her."

"Well, she does. And I'm sure she misses going out with Jake, but you should have asked me first."

"I'm sorry, Angel. You're right. I apologize for placing you in an awkward position, and it will never happen again." Bill meant every word. He had not realized he had spoken out of place. This was Angel's house and she was Angel's daughter and he was nobody…just a guy. "Do you want me to leave?"

Angel screwed her face up. "Of course not! I just don't want you to go over my head. I don't mean to sound harsh but it's the way I do things."

Angel turned and busied herself at the counter. Bill turned as well and walked back to the living room. He was just about to mention to Mae that he figured her mom didn't want her to go, when Angel was right behind him.

"Mommy?"

Angel passed Bill's coffee mug to him, then turned towards her daughter. "Yes, Mae, you may go. Are you finished your cake?"

"Yes, Mommy."

"Then scoot up and get your gear on."

Bill dropped in a chair, relief surging through his body. He would have to be careful with this woman. Now he knew what people meant when they talked about redheads.

Bill dug into his cake. "This is delicious, Angel, I certainly didn't expect a treat like this today. Sometime would you and Mae like to go out for dinner?"

Angel sat across from him eating her cake. She smiled. "It sounds like fun."

They no more had finished up the cake when Mae was clumping down the stairs. She was dressed from head to foot, even had her helmet on. She stood before them. "I'm ready."

Bill laughed. "I guess that's my cue to get my a…, rear up." Angel shot him a glance, but she didn't look angry. He would have to be careful how he talked around Mae. He wasn't used to children.

Soon they were both clumping out the door, Mae with an excited smile on her face, giving her mom a hug. Bill was tempted to do the same, but restrained himself with Mae present.

Angel watched as the snowmobile started up and roared away. She was comfortable with Mae going out with Bill, and she was happy that Mae wanted to go. It was a good sign, hopefully meaning that she was accepting having him around.

****

Bill decided to take the path behind Angel's house that led up into the woods. He could see when he hadn't gone too far that other roads led into it and there were snowmobile tracks. He thought about following it, but instead he pulled over and idled the machine.

"Have you been on this road before, Mae?" he called back to her.

"Yes, of course."

"Where does it go?"

"Well, many places probably, but it takes you to Aunt May's house."

"Oh, it does. Just go straight?"

"Yes, stay on the main road."

Bill gunned the motor and they took off again. It was a great day, the terrain was varied, a few bumps here and there but mostly smooth riding. When Bill reached an opening and came onto a field, he assumed he must be at the manor property. He took off full throttle, flying through the powder. He hoped that Mae was not frightened. He had no idea how fast Jake had ever gone with the girls on back, but he wasn't hearing her complaining.

They crested a hill and Bill saw the stately manor looking pristine in the crisp, clean snow. It was hard to tell from the outward view what was really going on inside the gutted interior. And since a few inches of snow had fallen overnight, a lot of tire tracks from workers and machines were covered up.

Bill rounded the manor and cut the motor just around the back. He waited for Mae to get off then it was his turn. He pulled off his helmet and saw a puff of cold air exit from Mae's mouth. "Now, that was fun!"

Her cheeks were rosy and her eyes were bright. Bill was glad he'd gotten to take her on the ride. "I had no idea your place was so close to the manor. You guys must have used this trail a lot to visit your aunt May."

"Sometimes," Mae said. "Want to see our snowmobile?"

"Sure."

Mae led him over to the old building behind the manor. The door was locked up with a bar over it. Mae attempted to push it, but it seemed stuck. Bill asked her to move back. He gave it one hard push upward with his hand and it let go. The door creaked as Bill yanked it open. It was a bit dark inside, but sunlight was creeping through the boards on the walls, letting enough light in to see.

"There it is." Mae pointed to a tarp and ran over and yanked it off the machine.

"Hey, that was a nice one in its day. It's smaller than some; I can see why you would like to ride it."

"It's an Arctic Cat. It's easy to drive, but Mommy says no. She thinks

I'm a baby. And anyway, there's no room for it now at home, with Daddy's new one there."

"Your dad has another one?"

"Yep, he just got it last spring. He only had it out a couple times." She looked at him with sad eyes. "I hope when Rachael comes home we can go out again. I hope there's still snow in March."

"Wouldn't it be more convenient if it was at your house?"

"Yeah."

Bill was about to volunteer taking it over some time, but then he remembered what had happened earlier. He would mention it to Angel before he ever said anything to Mae. He had learned his lesson.

"Have you been in the manor since they started working?" Bill asked.

"Nope. I don't like it, too messy."

"Yeah, but I think you'd enjoy seeing all the improvements that have been made already."

"I don't want to."

Bill was not about to push it any further. They left the old barn, locked up the door and traced their steps back to the snowmobile.

****

Angel had supper almost ready when the two snowmobilers arrived back. She had just placed a casserole in the oven and was making biscuits. The door opened and she was pleased to hear laughter. Angel left her biscuits and went to the door. "Hey, you two. Mae, your cheeks are so rosy. Did you have fun?"

Mae grinned at her mother while pulling off her boots. "He went fast."

"Oh?" Angel gave Bill a look but said no more. "Then I guess you had fun."

"I did." Mae gathered up her gear and started up the stairs. She paused and looked back at her mother. "When's supper? I'm starving."

"Soon. You go get cleaned up now."

Angel turned her attention to Bill. "So you went fast, eh?"

"Not really. She didn't seem to mind, if she had I would have slowed down. Really, Angel, it was perfectly safe."

"Okay, I'm not going to get into it. I guess I have to trust your judgement."

Bill looked annoyed. "You don't have to."

"I don't want to argue, Bill. You're back safe and sound and that's what matters. I have supper ready, are you staying?"

"Is that an invitation?"

Angel shook her head. "Really, Bill, you shouldn't be so sensitive. I'm just being a mother and looking out for my child."

Bill stood stiffly in the foyer. "And I'm not used to the third degree all the time."

"I'm sorry. I'm a little bit overprotective."

"You think?" Bill grinned.

"Well, would you like to stay for supper, Bill, or not?"

"Yes, Angel, that would be nice. I'm starving too."

Angel returned to the kitchen to finish her biscuits and Bill followed.

"Want a glass of wine?"

"No thanks, I'm driving."

Angel laughed. "Okay, you got me. Tea then?"

"Juice would be good."

"Try the fridge, you'll find a variety in there."

Bill got up and walked to the fridge and peeked inside. He pulled out a carton of orange juice and walked to the cupboard and found a glass.

"So, where did you go on your ride?"

"We ended up over at the manor. I had no idea there was such a direct path from here to there until Mae told me."

"How was Mae?"

"She was great." Bill put the juice back and took his glass to the counter, where he pulled out a stool and sat watching Angel make the biscuits.

"So, you two got along okay?"

"Yeah. She wanted to show me Jake's snowmobile. She also told me that Jake had a new one here. Mae's not happy that the old one that she likes is not over here instead of the new one. She said that Jake used to let her drive the old one around the place here."

"Yes, that's true, while he was watching her. He was very protective of his daughters also."

"Well, I was thinking, but I never mentioned this to Mae, learned my lesson earlier, that if you would like I could bring the old machine over and take the other back there, so when Rachael gets home she and Mae can have some fun on it without having to drive to the manor every time."

Angel was quiet as she formed the biscuits, as if she were thinking deeply.

Bill grew uneasy and wished he hadn't brought it up. "Of course, it's just a suggestion. It's totally up to you."

"I think it's a good idea. I think the girls would appreciate it. And no one but Jake has ever driven the new one, seems silly for it to be parked over here, even though the storage area is much better than over at the old barn."

"Won't hurt the machine, they're made for outdoors and harsh weather and cold."

Angel placed the biscuits in the oven and turned to Bill. "Then it's settled. Whenever you get time, you can do that. Thank you for offering."

Bill was taken aback slightly. One minute Angel seemed to be judging him over whatever he did, and in the next she was thanking him. He was confused, but then again he never did learn to understand women, starting back with his own mother.

"You're more than welcome, Angel. Don't you know by now, I'd do almost anything for you?"

Angel reddened. "Almost anything?"

"Well, yeah, I wouldn't walk on hot coals for you, or swim across a freezing lake. And there are probably a few other things I wouldn't do either, but seriously, I just want to make your life easier, if I can."

Angel took a seat beside him but looked away. Her expression was hard to read and Bill was hoping he hadn't stepped over some kind of line with her again. Suddenly she turned and looked into his eyes. She wore a wistful expression and he wasn't sure if it was sad or thoughtful, but he was about to find out.

Her hand went over his and she replied, "I don't know what I'd do without you in my life, Bill."

He was shocked. This was more than he had expected to hear right now or maybe ever. He was at a loss for words and didn't know how to respond to that. He decided to be casual. "I'm not going anywhere, unless you kick my ugly ass out."

Angel drew back. "Bill! You know, you've got to watch yourself in this house. I have a young impressionable daughter."

Bill laughed. "I know, Angel, but she's upstairs. Lighten up."

"I'm kidding, Bill. I guess we really don't know each other that well, do we?"

"We've got a lot to learn. And it should be fun doing so." He was about to give Angel a hug when he noticed a shadow in the hallway, and Mae appeared in the kitchen doorway. Bill drew back and the timer went off. Angel jumped up and pulled her biscuits out of the oven.

"Just in time, darling," she said to Mae. Come sit. Supper is ready."

****

After supper, Mae went into the family room to watch TV. Bill helped Angel clean up in the kitchen.

"You're pretty good on kitchen help," she said.

"I've had a lot of experience lately."

"I'm glad that Mae seemed to enjoy the snowmobile outing today. It was nice to see her all rosy and smiling again."

"You know, when I came over here, my intent was to ask you to go for a ride, but when I saw how interested Mae was I thought it might help our relationship."

Angel turned from the cupboard. "Well, she did seem to enjoy herself. I think we're done in here." Angel walked to the living room and Bill started getting his gear on. "You're leaving? So soon?"

"Yep. It's a fair ride back home so I'd better get going. Great supper, Angel. Thanks for inviting me."

Angel smiled. "I hope there isn't as much flack over it as the first time I invited you. By the way, Tanya sort of apologized for her behaviour at the coffee shop. She said she needed to apologize to you."

"No need. I do understand she has a lot on her plate. I'm glad though that she's come to terms with things as far as you're concerned."

Angel stood close to him. "I am also. It was most uncomfortable."

Bill reached for her and pulled her to him. His hug was comforting but he didn't stop there. He kissed her and as quickly pulled away. "Probably see you soon at the manor. Things are looking up over there." He opened the door and was gone.

Angel's hand flew to her mouth, touching her lips that had been touched by his. She smiled and went to the window to watch him as he rode down the lane.

CHAPTER THIRTEEN

The following week, Angel spent every day at the manor. Her living quarters on the top floor was really taking shape. The new kitchen was already together, except for the appliances that would be fitted in. The new bathroom fixtures were in place, including her new whirlpool. It was one of her favourite things when she moved into Jake's house and she wanted another.

The girls' rooms were rewired as was the rest of the house, but that was about all that was done to them yet. Angel wanted their input for colour schemes, but she had yet to tell either of them of her plans to move there. That would happen when Rachael came home for Easter.

By Friday, Angel was weary. She stayed at the manor almost every day until two thirty, when she left to be home before Mae returned from school. Mae didn't seem to have any interest in going to the manor to see what was going on there. Angel was talking to a carpenter in the manor's big kitchen about the cabinets, when Bill walked in.

"Hey, where have you been all week? Thought you were coming over?"

"Well," Bill replied, "I didn't really have a purpose, except to see you." He winked at her and they walked into the living room which was empty of workers. "You look tired, Angel."

"Oh, I'm fine. I've been here every day, but it's worth it. Things are really coming together."

"I think you need a break. A little ice fishing would be relaxing, you up for it?"

"When?"

"How about tomorrow?" Angel hesitated, and he continued, "You and Mae of course. I bet she would have fun."

"Well, I'll have to ask her. She has definite ideas about what she does and does not like to do lately."

"Oh, since I'm here, would you like me to take the snowmobile over to your place and bring the other one back here?"

Angel looked at her watch. "I have to go home soon. Mae will be getting off the school bus."

"That's okay. I'll take it over right now. You don't have to stay."

"I'll get going then and meet up with you over there."

****

Angel got home a few minutes before the bus. She was in the kitchen when Mae arrived. Mae shrugged out of her coat and kicked off her boots She grabbed up her backpack and had her foot on the bottom stair tread when her mother stuck her head out of the kitchen. "Mae, can you wait a minute, please? I want to talk to you about something."

Mae sighed. "What?"

"Oh, don't give me that look, it's nothing horrible. We've been invited to go ice fishing. What do you think of that?"

Mae screwed up her face. "Ice fishing? What's that?"

"Just what it sounds like, I guess. Fishing through the ice."

"I...dunno. Where?"

"Up at the lake...Bill's lake." Mae hesitated, as if she wasn't sure what to say, but Angel cut in, "I think it might be fun. I've never done it. And it's always fun to try something new."

"I guess."

"So? You game?"

"I guess."

"Good. I'll tell Bill we'll go. That's him now. He's bringing the old snowmobile over so you and Rachael can use it when she comes home."

Mae's eyes lit up. "He is?"

Angel saw the gleam in her daughter's eyes. Mae dropped her backpack on the step and went to the window to look out. "Can I go out?"

"No. He isn't staying. He's taking the new machine back to the manor."

"Oh." Mae returned to the stairs and grabbed up her backpack. "I better do my homework and get it out of the way."

Angel went out through the inside garage door and saw Bill exchanging snowmobiles.

He looked up. "Hey. I've never driven anything quite as fancy as this new one. It's a mighty powerful looking machine."

"Before you go, Bill, I talked to Mae, and she's up for the ice fishing."

"Wow. That's encouraging. I'm glad. Can you come around eleven? Gonna be a sunny day, we want to get out on the ice while the sun has some warmth."

"Sounds like a plan."

"And, Angel, wear your snowmobile suits. Bring your sunglasses, it's bright out there. And bring something hot to drink, and some snacks. It can get boring sometimes waiting for the fish to bite."

"Anything else?"

He walked towards her and put his arms around her. He whispered in her ear. "The thought of having you all to myself for the whole afternoon on the lake is more than enough."

Angel laughed. "We won't be alone. And maybe that's a good thing."

He smiled and brushed a strand of hair from her forehead. "I intend to get you alone one of these days. I'm a patient man."

Angel was at a loss for words, mixed feelings ran through her. But Bill didn't linger, he was on the new machine and out of there in no time, and she was standing in the garage alone. She looked over at the old snowmobile and thought of Jake. So much had changed in one short year. She never had been a big fan of snowmobiling, but the girls loved it. Jake had been determined that she learn to ride it so she did, but she never took it out herself.

She went back into the kitchen and thought about the next day. It would be an interesting time. She just hoped that Mae got something out of it. It would be a new experience for both of them.

****

Angel was up early. The workers would not be at the manor today so she had no need to go over there. She packed a few snacks and filled a big thermos with hot chocolate.

Mae seemed excited and before long they were in the car and on their way to the lake. Mae had never been there before so she was busy looking out the window and asking questions about where Mr. Canton lived.

"You can call him, Bill, darling, and he has a very lovely cabin. You'll like it."

When they arrived, there was no one around. Angel and Mae got out and walked up to the veranda. It looked the same as it did the day Angel had been there before, but now there were no plants. Angel knocked on the door. She waited then began to wonder where Bill was. She knocked again then heard a scratching sound. It was coming from the inside of the cabin.

"What's that noise?" Mae wanted to know.

Before Angel could reply, she heard Bill calling. She turned to see him walking towards the cabin.

He caught up to them and said, "You're early. It's just ten thirty."

"Yes, I guess we are. We were excited to get here."

Bill laughed. "Hi, Mae. Hope you're gonna have fun today."

Mae said nothing, just stepped back from the door. Her mother did the same. As Bill opened the door he was almost knocked over when a black streak zoomed by him, ran out into the year and started running around in circles.

Bill laughed. "He does this every time I leave the place. You'd think I was gone for a month. Come here, boy." The almost black dog ran around in circles, his long skinny tail up in the air over his back. He suddenly stopped and crouched down on his front paws with his rear up in the air, the tail flapping back and forth over his back.

Mae laughed, and Angel remarked, "I didn't know you had a dog.

Where was he when I was here before?"

Bill called the dog to his side. It had finally quieted down. "I just got him."

"What kind of dog is he?" Mae wanted to know.

"He's a mutt, sort of a black lab-pointer combination." Bill fluffed the dog's fur and patted his head. "One of my neighbours had him but he's old and his family just took him to a nursing home, so I was approached would I like to have this lovely, mangy six- month-old dog."

After they all went inside, Mae made instant friends with Ralph. It was warm and cozy inside the cabin, and Angel could have curled up beside the welcoming fire and read all afternoon. But she was game for the fishing expedition as well and went back out to the car to bring in their heavy outer wear.

After they had all geared up in warm clothing, they gathered up their drinks and snacks, and Mae piled them all in her backpack that she had brought along. "Is Ralph coming with us?" she asked, pointing to the dog.

"Not this time," Bill replied. "I've only had him a few days and he's not had much training. I really don't trust him out for a long time, until we get to know each other better. I think we'd have more fun fishing if he were to stay here."

They made their way outside and waited while Bill went to the shed. He returned with some fishing rods and a backpack of his own slung over his shoulder. "You guys can take the fishing poles. I'll handle the other stuff." They headed around the back of the cabin and followed the same wood's path that Angel and Bill had taken when they'd gone out on the boat.

They arrived at the lake shore and walked out onto the ice. "Are you sure this is safe?" Angel asked.

"With the cold weather we've been having this winter? Pretty much so."

Mae ran ahead then stopped and came back. "There are big holes out there."

"Yep, how'd you think we were gonna fish?"

"How'd you do that?"

"I did it just before you guys arrived. That's where I was. I sometimes use an ice saw, but I just bought a hand auger and it worked great today."

They reached the ice holes and Mae peeked down one of them. "I saw a fish."

"The fish don't swim deep in the winter. They're right under the ice, only about a foot or two down."

"You've got seats." Mae laughed and sat in front of one of the ice holes. "How do I fish?" she wanted to know.

Bill stood with his hands on his hips and grinned at her. "Hey, don't get ahead of yourself now, be patient."

Angel sat on another box and waited for Bill to show them what to do. "What's our bait this time?"

"Night crawlers," Bill replied. "Some people prefer minnows, but minnows are squirmy and being that it's so shallow, they sometimes like to try and come back up the hole. So I like night crawlers. I get them from a worm farm not far from here. That's where I got the wooden boxes for sitting. They use these boxes for homes for the worms."

Angel thought it was all very interesting and watched as Bill pulled a container out of his backpack and took the lid off. He held it towards Mae and she peeked inside.

"Yuk, worms."

Bill laughed. "Yep, and you're gonna put it on your hook."

Mae made a fuss, but she was grinning. "No, I'm not." She shook her head.

"Then your mom can do it for you."

Bill had another container that he opened and reached inside. He pulled out a few bits of something and sprinkled it in the hole.

"What's that?" Mae asked.

"It's night crawlers, but they're chopped up. That's called chumming. It sort of gets the fish excited. I don't drop much or they won't be hungry when we fish."

"Why are these fishing poles so short?" Angel asked. "Don't look like what we used on the boat."

"Nope. These are jig poles. We'll be jigging today. That's how you ice fish."

"Complicated," Angel said.

"Not really. You'll get the hang of it."

"I want to fish," Mae added.

"You ladies are really impatient. So, let's get your jig poles suited up. These bright coloured things are called lures or jigs, and this is your treble hook, see it has three points. So you take a night crawler and hook it a couple of times, like this, sort of loop it through so it dangles, then lower the line until it's just below the ice. You can see the end of the ice here."

Mae took a look. She was paying extreme attention to Bill.

"Then you just sit there and lift the pole every now and then, like this, that's called jigging, and when you get a bite, you pull the line out and voilà you got yourself a fish." Bill handed the jig pole to Mae. "Go to 'er."

Mae grinned at Bill. "Thought I was going to put the worm on."

"You can next time," Bill replied.

Angel had been watching also. She already had taken a night crawler from the can and was looping it on her jig pole hook.

Bill dumped the contents of his backpack on the ice. He pulled out a long flat wooden thing that looked to Angel something like a stick with a flag on it. She already had her rod baited so she slipped it into one of the holes and jigged it, like she'd seen Bill demonstrate. "What in the world is that, Bill?"

Bill scooped the rest of the stuff back in the backpack, then got up and walked over to Angel. "This is a tip-up. It's what I'll be using today." He showed her the piece of wood with the spool of line attached to it. There was a thin piece of metal that went from the spool to the flag. "You put the line on the spool and put the swivel at the end of the line, then the fishing line with the hook is attached to the swivel. Add a night crawler and put the hook with the bait under the ice, set the tip-up right over the ice hole and wait. Of course you have to lift it once in a while, my form of jigging. When a fish comes along and latches on, the flag is lifted and you know you've got one."

Angel turned to her hole and jigged a bit. "I'm anxious to see it working."

Bill put a night crawler on the hook and set the tip-up over the third ice hole. "How are you doing, Mae?" he asked.

"It's boring."

"Well, that's why you have your snacks." He took hold of Mae's line so she could get her backpack. Mae pulled out a large thermos and placed it on the ice beside her mom's ice hole. She then found some snacks and came back to her own wooden box. She took the line from Bill and gave him a smile.

Bill was thinking the day was working out pretty well. He had wanted to get closer to Mae for a long time. He had just not known how to do it. For one thing, he had never been around kids much. His ex-wife, Lorraine, had a brother who had a daughter, and there were times when they used to visit. He had enjoyed interacting with her, but that was short lived.

Mae's bag of chips went flying through the air. "Something's happening!" she shouted. Bill turned from watching his tie-up and saw Mae pulling on her line.

"You got one?" he called. "Just pull the line in." He went over to have a look. "That's it, you got one all right. Now give it a good yank up." The fish slipped out on the ice, twisting and flopping around. "That's a big fellow," Bill remarked and grabbed the fish with his hand to quiet it and move it farther from the ice hole. "Good girl."

Mae was beaming as she stood up to take a look at her catch. They were all standing over the fish, when Bill picked it up and took the hook out. He had a bucket nearby and plopped the fish in it. He turned to Mae and gave her a hug. "You did good, girl. I'm proud of you." They did a high five and Mae went dancing around the ice.

"Be careful, Mae," Angel called. "Don't want to step into one of those holes."

Mae quieted down and Bill handed her a night crawler to bait her line. "You might just be the lucky one today. See if you can get another." Mae settled down, looking serious above her line. She tackled the worm. She was not bored anymore.

"What's going on with that flag, Bill?" Angel asked.

Bill looked over then went to his tie-up, pulling it out of the water. "I got a little feller of my own on here." He pulled the line up and grabbed the trout. It was smaller than Mae's. "Come on little guy, join your buddy in the bucket."

Bill set up his tie-up again and placed it over the ice hole. "It's your turn now, Angel."

"I'm not having much luck, here. I don't even think I got a bite yet."

"You'd know if you did."

"I got another," Mae yelled, pulling on the line. She had it on the ice in no time.

Bill grabbed it, removed the hook and stuck it in the bucket. "You're on a roll, girl, fantastic!"

Mae looked up at him. Her cheeks were rosy and her smile was wide and gleeful. She giggled. "This is fun."

Angel opened the thermos and had a cup of hot chocolate. "You extremely lucky fish catchers like to have some hot chocolate, or are you just too busy catching fish?"

"I wouldn't mind," Bill replied and placed a cup in front of the thermos for Angel to pour. He stood beside Angel sipping the hot drink, while watching Mae jig her line. He looked down at Angel and whispered, "She's good."

They fished another half hour and Mae said, "My feet are getting cold."

"Do you girls want to call it a day?"

Angel rose and pulled her line out of the water. The little night crawler was still dangling on the end. "That sounds good to me. I'm feeling cramped, sitting so long."

Bill looked over. "How about you, Mae? You ready to quit?"

Mae yanked her line out of the water and got up. "Yep. Can we eat the fish?"

Bill looked at Angel. "That's up to your mother. You guys can take them home or we can cook them up here."

"Can we, Mom?" Mae was anxiously looking at her mother for a positive answer.

"I don't see why not."

They gathered up their gear, and started back to the shore. Mae noticed a long rope and asked, "What's that doing out here?"

"See that big tree over there?" Bill pointed to a very large pine tree on the shoreline. "If you follow this rope, you'll see that it's attached to that tree. That rope always goes out on the lake with me, and if there's any trouble, I have a life line. It's better not to fish alone, but when you're a loner like me, you do it."

Mae carried her fishing rod and the bucket with the fish in it. Angel had her own rod and Mae's backpack slung across her shoulder. Bill walked behind the girls with his own backpack and carried his tie-up. He watched and listened as mother and daughter made small talk, and he was pleased to hear their laughter ring out in the afternoon air.

Back at the cabin, Bill laid the fish on several layers of newspaper on the counter. He picked up each trout by the tail and scraped them forward several times with a sharp knife to remove the gills. He then tossed the fish into the sink and asked Mae if she wanted to watch how to clean them. Mae was all eyes and ears. She had been playing with Ralph, but jumped up from the floor to see what Bill was going to do.

After rinsing the fish, Bill got out a long knife with a good point on the end. "We'll do your big guy first. You have to have a sharp knife. Turn the fish over and find the vent on the belly and insert knife." He slid it easily up the belly of the fish and stopped just at the two fins before the head.

"You leaving the head on?" Mae asked.

"For now, and there's a very good reason. Watch." Bill placed the fish on a cutting board, and inserted the knife behind the head. He cut half way. "Only going through the back bone, you'll see why in a minute." Bill laid down his knife, picked up the fish and pulled down on the head.

"Euuu." Mae grimaced.

The fins and entrails came out in one fell swoop. "There, isn't that easy?"

"What about the bones?"

"We'll get to that later. There's more to do here first." Bill opened the fish, took his thumb and ran it down inside the belly. "It's being a little stubborn," he said. "So, I'll just take the tip of the knife here. See what I'm doing? That's the blood line and we need to get it out of there." He ran the tip of the knife along the bloodline and it opened, blood spurting forth. He laid down the knife and cleaned the blood out with his thumb.

"There, you have a nice clean fish. We'll just do the other two. Angel, look in the top cupboard and you'll find some rice. I think it might be nice to have a pot of rice to go with our fish."

Angel had been watching also, from a distance. She came forward and got the rice down. "Where should I find a pot, Bill?"

"Try the lower door near the stove."

Angel found what she was looking for and proceeded to draw water for the rice.

Mae was hypnotically taken by the cleaning procedure. She watched as Bill expertly gutted the other two fish. "Look, Mae, the night crawler you used to catch the big guy is still alive in the guts."

Mae looked at the mess of intestines and saw the crawling worm. "Neat. You keeping him?"

Bill laughed. "I don't think so. We've got lots of fresh ones left over." He dropped the last fish into the sink where the other two were lying, and scooped up the heads and entrails and wrapped all of it in the newspapers.

Mae peeked in the sink. "What about the tails, you forgot to cut them off."

"Oh, no I didn't. The tails are good. You wait, when these are all cooked up, you'll find the tails are nice and crispy."

"Eat the tails?" She shivered.

"You don't have to," Bill said. "More for me."

Mae changed her mind. "Okay, I'll try them. What's next?"

Bill was delighted to see Mae so interested. "What's next is that we get the frying pan on, stick some butter in there, and we're ready to fry up our fish."

"Mmmm." Mae licked her lips in anticipation of the tasty trout.

Bill got out a frying pan and slid some butter into it. He got the heat going and when it was hot enough, he placed the three fish into the pan. He grinned to himself as he watched Mae from the corner of his eye, staring at the fish in the pan.

After a few minutes of sizzling, he turned the fish. He then added salt and pepper. "I don't like to overpower my fish with spices," he said.

Angel had been looking around the cupboards and found what she was looking for. She set up the table and made a big pot of tea. She checked on the rice which looked fluffy and appealing.

"I'd say we're just about done here," Bill said, while flipping over the trout. He turned and saw Angel standing by the table. "Hey, you've got us all set up. Let's eat."

Mae sat willingly at the table, watching Bill's every move. Bill slid a fish in everyone's plate, giving the biggest one to Mae. "After all, you did catch two of them."

"No," Mae said. "You take the big one, you're the biggest."

Bill laughed. "If you say so."

Angel started to dish out the rice, but Bill stopped her. "Not yet. If you're not wanting to be chewing on bones, here's a good way to debone your fish."

"We're taking the bones out now?" Mae asked.

"Yep," Bill told her. "It's easier after they're cooked. Watch and learn. I'm not doing this part for you."

Angel and Mae had their eyes glued to Bill to see what he would do next.

"Pick up the little fellow by the tail, slide your fork under the meat part at the end, and carefully pull down on it. See how this part's falling away and you're hanging onto the spine and the bones? There." The piece of fillet fell gently in the plate. "Now, turn it over and do the same thing." The other fillet lifted from the backbone. "You got yourself some nice chunks of fish without the bones. Okay, your turn."

Angel picked up her fish by the tail and Mae followed suit. Bill watched as they carefully repeated what he had done. When the pieces of boneless fish fell into their plates, they were both left holding a backbone with lots of bones attached.

"Cool," Mae remarked.

Bill laughed. "Okay, we're now ready for the rice." Angel started to jump up, but Bill put a hand out. "I'll get it, Angel."

Ralph padded over to the table and sat in front of Angel. "Oh, look at that little face," she said. "But I'm not going to feed you, no matter how much you beg."

After the rice had been distributed, Bill made Ralph go sit on the rug in the living room. "He's got a lot to learn, but he does sit well."

Bill rejoined Angel and Mae at the table. The two females had already devoured most of their trout. He thought it had been an incredible day, so far, and it almost looked like a family to him. But dare he even think such things?

CHAPTER FOURTEEN

Angel was pleased with the way the fishing expedition had turned out. Mae seemed in a good mood on the way home and talked a lot about the fishing, the dog, and Bill also.

"So, it sounds like you really liked ice fishing, Mae."

"Yeah, it was cool."

"Maybe we can do it again sometime."

Mae nodded. "I'd like to see Ralph again also. He's such a cute puppy."

Angel smiled as they turned into their driveway.

It was beginning to snow lightly and she was glad she had headed for home when she did. Inside, they unpacked their gear and Mae went up to her room. No doubt to draw fish, Angel thought.

She had barely gotten inside and stashed stuff away when the phone rang. It was Bill calling to see if they got home okay.

Angel's heart leapt in her chest. "Hi, Bill, we just go in."

"Yes, I thought you'd be there by now."

"It's snowing again."

"Can't seem to stop now, can it?"

"Well, Mae doesn't mind. She's waiting for Rachael to come home so they can take the snowmobile out. But that won't be until April so unless she can come some weekend, I'm afraid the weather might be too warm by then, and Mae will be disappointed."

"Did you girls have a good time today?"

"Oh, Bill, Mae never stopped talking about it all the way home, and she's in love with your dog."

Bill laughed.

"I'm so happy that Mae had a good time, and I couldn't believe how she opened up to you."

"How about her mom? Did you have a good time?"

"I did, I really did. Thank you for inviting us and for the fishing lesson as well. We never bothered much with the fish once they were caught, when we used to be on the sailboat. I guess Jake took care of that, all we did was eat them." Angel laughed.

Bill laughed again. "Glad you enjoyed it. I can't remember when I've had so much fun fishing. I won't keep you; I just wanted to be sure you got home safely."

After Angel got off the phone she went upstairs to see how Mae was doing. She was surprised to see that Mae was using her laptop and not drawing. Angel glanced at the screen and saw fish. She smiled. It looked like

Mae was doing some research. It was nice to see her daughter interested in life again.

Angel drew a bath and settled into the bubbly, hot foam. She was developing new feeling for Bill Canton. She felt that he might turn out to be more than just a friend. If the past afternoon's activities were any indication of future outings, she could see a bright future ahead.

It was hard to believe that just a few short months ago, she had not even wanted to live anymore. If not for her children needing her, she had not at that time found any reason to go on. But now there was promise in the future, not only with the retreat, which excited her greatly, but also with whatever was forming between her and Bill Canton. Now that Mae seemed to have taken a liking to him, she didn't foresee any obstacles in their path.

She leaned her head back on the bath pillow and sighed, feeling light as a breeze for the first time in ages.

****

Near the end of March, Angel received a call from Rachael telling her that she had no classes on Friday, so she would be home early in the day for the weekend. Angel was excited. Rachael had not been home since Christmas.

When Rachael arrived, there was still snow on the ground. It seemed like it might never let up this year. Angel had a nice dinner planned, and Bill had been invited as well.

"Oh, it's so good to be home," Rachael remarked at the dinner table.

"It's wonderful to have you home, Rachael," Angel replied. "Have you made any summer plans yet?"

"Well, I still haven't decided. I've been looking into summer work in Truro. There's an animal clinic there that will be hiring. I've already talked to them and it seems promising. But then I would really like to be home, so while I'm here I'm going to check out some clinics in the area and see if there might be a chance for me getting on somewhere."

"I hope you get to work here," Mae put in.

Bill raised a glass. "Here's to lucrative summer employment, Rachael, wherever it may be."

"Bill and I were going over to the manor tonight, would you girls like to come along and see what's been done over there?"

"No, Mom," Rachael said. "I mean, I want to, but I'm getting together with Katie and Beth over at Dean's house. We're going out then meet up with some others."

Bill rose from the table. "Have fun, Rachael...while you're young."

Rachael gave Bill a smile and got up also. She and Mae left the dining room and went upstairs. Bill hung around the kitchen and helped Angel clean up. After the dishes were all stacked, Angel poured more wine and walked into the living room. Bill was behind her.

"I thought we were going over to the manor."

Angel kicked her shoes off and settled on the sofa. "Well, the girls seem to be busy so maybe I'll wait until tomorrow. And Mae is always reluctant to go over there."

"Is there something you wanted to do at the manor?"

Angel took a sip of her wine and smiled at him. "No. Nothing that can't wait." She patted the sofa seat beside her for Bill to sit down.

Just as Bill was joining her, Rachael came down the stairs and into the living room. "Nice to see you again, Bill. Mom, I won't be late, at least I don't think I will."

"Well, if you're driving, be careful."

"I will, Mom." She kissed her mother on the cheek and left.

"She's a great girl, Angel, always in a good mood."

"Yes, she gets that from her father. I don't ever recall Jake having moody times. But Mae is a different story. She's like Jake in many ways but she has her moods. I guess she gets that from me."

"You? I've never seen you in a bad mood. Except at the grocery store."

"Let's not go there. I wasn't in a bad mood. I was just upset with you and couldn't understand why you were acting like you were. But, I guess we talked that out."

"Yep. Now we understand each other."

Angel gave him a look. "We do?"

Bill hunched his shoulders and looked confused. "I thought we did."

"Well, I'm not so sure. I'm still having a hard time trying to figure out where you and I are going."

"I thought we were going to just let it be and see where it takes us."

"Yes, I know we said that. But—"

"But you're having second thoughts?"

Angel finished her wine and set the glass on the coffee table. "I don't know what I'm thinking. I'm almost as confused as I was when I first came to Nova Scotia to help my aunt."

"What do you mean?"

Angel got up and left the room. She brought the wine bottle back with her and filled her glass and Bill's. She took a drink then continued, "I was a mess when I came here. My aunt was in a fix. She needed help to run the Bed and Breakfast. You didn't know Aunt May but she was a very independent person. One day she was outside painting the trim on her windows. She fell off a ladder and broke her leg. That's when she called me, all in dither because she needed help."

"And you came running?"

"I was off for the summer so, yeah. Anyway, that's when I met Jake. Well, for the second time. When I was a kid, I had a big crush on him, but he was older and had lots of girlfriends then. He barely noticed me. But Aunt May asked him to pick me up at the airport, and he did."

"So did he notice you that time?"

Angel laughed. "Our first meeting didn't go so well. He was late and I left him at the airport and rented a car."

"You left him? After he'd gone to the airport to pick you up?"

Angel laughed again. "I did. I was angry. After what I'd gone through with James, I wasn't about to let another man push me around."

"Just because he was late?"

"He was late because he had a business meeting. I'd been through that kind of stuff with James and I wasn't taking it anymore."

Bill poured more wine. "Well, I guess I won't ever be late when I'm meeting you somewhere."

"Oh, Bill. That's not the point. I was insecure and damaged. Someday I'll tell you about my marriage to James. That is if you want to hear it."

"Of course I want to hear it. I want to know everything that you want to tell me about you, Angel. I know one thing, you're an independent woman today and even though I offer you advice in business matters, I know that in the end you'll make your own decisions."

"I will," Angel was quick to reply. "But I never would have been in this place in my life if it hadn't been for Jake. His constant reassurance that I was a strong person finally got through to me. I leaned on him a lot over the years, but now that he's gone his strength has stayed with me."

Bill rose and walked across the room to the CD holder. He pulled one from the shelf and asked, "Mind if I play something?"

Angel rose as well. "No, please go ahead. I need to replace this bottle." She picked up the empty wine bottle and walked to the kitchen.

Bill chose *Romantic Classics* and the cut, *This Guy's in Love with You* by Julio Iglesias. He paused the player when Angel came back in the room. She walked over to him and asks, "Did you find something?" Bill held the CD jacket up for Angel to see. "Oh, that one."

Angel's hand trembled and the wine bottle wavered. Bill reached out and grabbed it. "You all right?"

"I'm...fine. That's Jake's CD."

"You don't want me to play it?"

Angel took the bottle from Bill and walked to the coffee table and filled their glasses. After she was finished she turned. "Go ahead, play it. It's a lovely CD. Jake and I danced to it many times."

Bill pressed play and walked over to Angel. She passed him a glass and he took it then set it back on the coffee table. He reached for her hand and asked, "Would you like to dance tonight?" Angel got up, still holding his hand. She gazed into his eyes and he saw tears there. As they began to move to the music, Bill asked softly, "Does this song make you sad?"

Angel answered in an almost indistinguishable voice. "It's Jake's favourite cut off the album. He loved that song."

Instantly, Bill wished he'd chosen another CD, but how was he to know? He liked the song himself, that's why he picked it. "I'm sorry. I didn't mean to bring back bad memories."

"They're not bad memories, they're good memories. Let's just dance."

As he held her in his arms, he could imagine her and Jake standing in that very same living room dancing closely just like they were now, and his gut filled with guilt.

Angel moved to the music and old memories rushed through her head. She wanted to be strong and not let it affect her, but it was getting to her. As they turned towards the stairway, she noticed Mae standing there.

"Mae? What is it, dear? I thought you'd be in bed." Mae turned and rushed up the stairs. Angel stopped dancing and pulled from Bill. "I've got to go to her."

Reaching the top of the stairs, Angel made her way to Mae's bedroom. Mae was already in bed. Angel sat on the bed and touched Mae's hair. "Are you okay, darling? Did you want to say good night to me?"

"Why are you dancing with him?" Mae's voice was flat.

"Well, it's just a dance, Mae. Don't you remember when daddy and I used to dance?"

"I do, but I don't think that you should be dancing with him."

"Don't be silly, Mae, it's no different than when we went ice fishing. It's just having some fun. Now go to sleep, and tomorrow you and Rachael and I will spend the day together, okay?" She tucked Mae in and kissed her forehead.

Upon returning to the living room, she saw that Bill had shut the CD player off and was sitting on the sofa with his drink.

"I'm sorry, Bill. I guess Mae was a bit upset that we were dancing. I have to say I'm feeling a bit guilty myself."

"You're not the only one."

"This is hard, isn't it? I guess we'll have to be careful when Mae's around, she's still very sensitive about her father."

Bill sighed and set his glass down. "Is this the way it's always going to be?"

"Bill!"

"Okay, okay, I get your point. Look it's late and time for me to leave. Thanks for dinner…and the dance."

"Bill, I'm sorry—"

"No need to be sorry. This *is* hard, but I'm trying to understand." He walked to the door, and just as he was about to open it, Rachael walked in.

"Oh, hi. You're still here?"

"Just leaving." Bill walked out the door that Rachael had just walked in.

"What's up with him?" Rachael looked questionably at her mother.

Angel hunched her shoulders. "Nothing."

Rachael removed her coat and boots and went into the living room to sit by her mother. "Come on, Mom. What do you mean nothing? He looked pissed, like you guys had been arguing or something."

"It wasn't an argument, far from it."

"Mom…spill it."

Angel poured another glass of wine and took a deep sigh. "Right after you left, we were just chatting about our lives, or I was mostly. I went out to get another bottle of wine and when I came in, he was playing a CD. It was your dad's, Julio Iglesias CD, the one he loved to play and we used to dance to. So, I told Bill that and he asked me to dance. Mae came downstairs and saw us and she got upset. Later, I told Bill that we would have to be careful around her as to what we did."

"Like what?"

"I don't know what you mean."

"Like careful doing what? What have you been doing except dancing?"

"Well, that's it, actually nothing much. Well, he did kiss me a few times."

Rachael sighed. "Oh, Mom, are you getting feelings for him?"

Angel rubbed her brow. "I don't know."

"Well, you either are or you aren't. It's pretty simple to know."

Angel shot an irritating glance at Rachael. "No. It's not simple, Rachael. In fact, it's very complicated, and made so by other people."

"What other people? If you like him, Mom and he likes you, then what other people matter?"

"You do…Mae does, Tanya does. You are all my family and your opinions matter to me. I do like Bill and I know he likes me, but it's mainly Mae. She doesn't seem to like him, no matter what I do or what Bill does. The day we went ice fishing I thought there was a breakthrough. Mae seemed to enjoy herself and she interacted well with Bill. He also was very good with her, and he seemed at ease with her around and all the questions that she always has. I was pleased."

"Then what happened?"

"Tonight Mae wanted to know why I was dancing with him. She said I shouldn't be. I told her it was just having fun and to go to sleep."

"Mae's a kid, Mom. It's hard for her to understand, and she feels like you're forgetting Dad."

Angel sighed. "I wish I could get through to her, but maybe she's just too young to understand."

Rachael put a hand on Angel's shoulder. "Don't worry about it, Mom, it'll all work out, you'll see."

Rachael smiled and hugged her mom. "You're a wonderful girl, Rachael. Sometimes I think about what my life would have been like had your father not taken a chance on me and asked me to become part of his and your life."

"And I'm glad that you're my mom. I sort of remember my real mom a bit, but mostly now it's just her pictures and what Dad and Aunt Tanya and Grampy and Grandma told me about her."

Angel hugged Rachael then got up. "I think it's time we called it a day. All that wine has made me sleepy." She stretched and yawned and picked up the wine bottle to return to the kitchen.

She and Rachael went upstairs and to their respective bedrooms. Before Rachael went to hers, Angel gave her another hug. "Thanks for the girl talk. It's nice to have someone to talk to who understands."

Rachael hugged her mother back and went to her room.

Angel proceeded to walk down the hall and into her own bedroom, the bedroom that she used to share with Jake. A lot of his belongings were still in the room. She would have to do something about that one day, but she didn't want to think about it. Thinking of parting with Jake's clothing and other personal possessions was just too painful…still.

She wondered why others didn't realize how very lonely she still was for Jake. Tanya had said that she understood, but then turned around and made remarks that hurt Angel. Mae was too young to consider and Angel totally got it as to why she reacted like she did. Angel did not know if Jake's parents had any inkling or not about what was going on with Bill Canton. She thought she would have to find out and decided that one of these days she would drive over there and see them. Then she realized that Jake's parents were not even at home. They spent considerable time away now that they were retired, and they had a place in Florida that they spent the winters. She would just have to wait until they returned, maybe not until May.

Angel was weary, she undressed and pulled a nightgown over her head and slid between the sheets. As she lay in her big bed alone she thought of her aunt May and what her aunt had told her one time. *You'll work it out, child. Love always finds a way.*

May had been talking about Angel and Jake's relationship at the time, when Angel had been so confused over whether she loved Jake or not, and whether he truly loved her.

"And it all worked out, Aunt May," Angel said out loud. "Oh, how I wish you were here right now to advise me on what to do about Bill Canton."

She turned on her side and stared into the darkness, thinking about

Bill. The way he'd left had disturbed her greatly. He hadn't even said a proper good night to her. Maybe he was just taken aback when Rachael walked in the door…or maybe not. She closed her eyes and decided that first thing in the morning she would call him and ask him to come by and bring his snowmobile. She hoped he would come and that the four of them could have some fun in the last of the snow. Angel drifted off to sleep, thinking of better days and hoping her aunt was right and that things would eventually work out and that love would find a way.

CHAPTER FIFTEEN

The morning was bright and sunny and Angel gave Bill a call right after breakfast.

"Hey," she said to him, "I guess you got home all right after all that wine last night."

"Oh, I did," he replied. "I don't believe I had as much as you did. Did you sleep well?"

"I certainly did, once I got to sleep."

"Something keeping you awake?"

Angel figured she might as well be to the point, much like he always was. "Actually, yes, there was something. I was thinking about the way you left last night, kind of sudden."

"Well, it was time. We weren't really getting anywhere in our conversation, at least it didn't seem that way to me."

Angel decided not to linger on the night before. "Well, we might get somewhere today, that is if you'll bring your snowmobile over. I thought the four of us could go out for a ride. I know that Mae would love it. I haven't approached them yet, but I'm sure there won't be a problem."

"Maybe you should ask them first and call me back."

"Bill."

"What?"

Angel sighed. "Okay, if that's what you want. Will you come though, if they agree?"

"Love to."

"Okay, I'll get back to you shortly."

Angel called the girls who were still sleeping as far as she knew. Before long they both came dragging down the stairs. Rachael looked tired. "What did you do last night?" Angel asked her.

"Hung out."

Angel figured that was about all the information she was going to get, so she continued on with stacking dishes while the girls ate breakfast. "Looks like a great day out there," Angel said. After no response from the girls who sat lazily munching cereal, she tried again. "Anyone like to take the snowmobile out today?"

Mae's eyes brightened. "Can we, Rachael?"

Rachael hesitated. "I kinda promised Aunt Tanya that I'd come over soon as I got home."

"You can do that tomorrow, Rachael," Angel said. "Today's such a great day and there might not be too many more, it's melting out there as we speak."

"Okay then," Rachael agreed.

Mae's toast popped and she grabbed it and buttered it, quickly shoving half of it in her mouth.

"Hey, what's the rush, Mae?"

"We want to get going soon."

Angel laughed. "You've got lots of time, it's only early. Besides I've ask Bill to bring his snowmobile over so we can all go out. I did promise you I'd spend the day with you girls, didn't I Mae?"

Mae nodded and didn't seem upset that Bill was coming over.

"Cool," Rachael remarked. "I'd like to see his machine."

"It's old," Mae commented, "but it's fast." She giggled, and Angel felt that both girls were in agreement with Bill coming over.

After they finished up their breakfast and went upstairs, Angel gave Bill a call back. Then she got her laptop and started looking up retreats. She would soon need to tell the workers what she wanted done to the old barn, and so far she didn't have a clue what it should look like.

An hour later, the girls were downstairs and getting their gear ready. "Come on, Mom, get off the Internet and get ready," Mae said.

"Bill isn't even here yet. You guys are just being impatient."

"Doesn't mean we can't go out and get started."

"Oh, no. We'll all go out together. So just settle down. If you want something to do, go empty the dishwasher."

Mae groaned, but Rachael put an arm around her shoulder and they trudged to the kitchen.

Before too long the sound of a snowmobile could be heard whining its way up the driveway. Angel jumped up and went to the window. She smiled when she saw Bill get off the snowmobile and take off his helmet.

She pulled the door open just as he reached the steps. "Hi."

Bill smiled at her and came inside, taking off his boots and jacket. "You were right, Angel. It's a perfect day for sledding."

Rachael and Mae, hearing the snowmobile, bounded down the steps. "Hi, Bill," Rachael said, her dimples showing deep in her cheeks. "You ready for a race?"

"Oh, no. No racing allowed," Angel cut in.

"Oh, Mom. You're no fun at all."

Mae stood behind Rachael, but she had a smile on her face and her eyes were bright.

"Okay everyone, let Bill get out of the way so you guys can get your suits on."

Bill sidestepped Mae who was yanking open the closet door. He decided he'd better go in the living room and sit down. After Angel and the girls got suited up, Bill came back to the foyer and put his jacket and boots on. "Is everyone ready?" he wanted to know.

"Yes, yes, yes." Mae giggled.

"Then we're off," Bill said, opening the door and letting the girls go out first.

The ride started off slowly as the two sleds wound their way back of the house and towards the woods road. Rachael was in the lead and Angel hoped that she wouldn't be silly and speed, trying to keep ahead of Bill. Usually Rachael was the sensible one and she was always careful driving whether it was the snowmobile or her car.

Bill revved the motor and the machine bounced over the snow-covered road. The sun was bright and Angel wished she'd brought along her sunglasses. Bill wore snowmobile goggles that were tinted, but he was driving so he got most of the wind. Angel was enjoying the ride and had forgotten how much fun it could be on the trails.

Rachael took a side trail so Bill followed. The trail winded around and eventually came back out on the original road. He assumed that Rachael had been on these trails before, so he was glad that she was leading. She was a good driver and she didn't speed. He imagined that Angel was relieved about that. Angel seemed very cautious in many respects, and he guessed that she probably had a right to be. He had never been a parent, so who was he to judge Angel on being over protective with her girls?

After a few more side trips onto other trails, Rachael returned to the main road and headed for home. They had been riding around for about an hour, and Angel was beginning to feel a bit cold across her shoulders. She reminded herself that the reason for that was probably that she had never been out much this past winter and wasn't used to the cold weather.

Both machines returned to the front yard and purred to a stop. Angel had barely gotten off the snowmobile before Mae was in front of her. "Can I go for a ride by myself, Mom, please?"

Angel hesitated, but Bill whispered to her, "Let her drive around the yard and up the hill. Jake let her didn't he? And he wouldn't have, if he hadn't thought that she could handle it."

Angel gave in and gave her permission. Mae jumped on the snowmobile and rode it around where they could watch her. After she had gone up the small hill and back down, Angel hollered to her, "That's enough." She motioned to Mae to come back.

Mae brought the snowmobile around and got off. Her face was rosy and she was smiling from ear to ear. "That was so fun, Mom, thanks for letting me go."

"You can thank Bill for that. He convinced me that you could handle the machine."

Mae smiled at Bill then walked behind Rachael towards the house. Angel gave Bill a glance and saw him winking at her. She walked up to him and linked arms. "I think you just made Mae a happy girl"

"Actually it was we. Without your consent my two cents worth would have been useless."

"Ah, but it was your two cents worth that convinced me."

Bill gave Angel a hug and pulled her closer. He whispered in her ear, "I can be very convincing at times, so stay tuned." Angel laughed but didn't pull away. It felt good to have someone's arm around her again.

They entered the foyer and heard the girls laughing in the kitchen. As they kicked off their boots and shed their coats, Rachael called, "We've got hot chocolate. Want some?"

"Umm, sounds good," Bill called back.

The girls were seated at the kitchen island, when Angel and Bill entered the kitchen. They all sat around making small talk in an easy way that Angel enjoyed. Why couldn't things always be this way? Why was heartache and misery always showing up at unexpected times? She decided to stop analyzing the day and just go with it. Wasn't that what Jake would do? After the hot chocolate and snacks were finished, Angel asked Bill if he'd like to stay for supper.

"You know I can't turn down a meal, Angel, especially when you're cooking."

The girls laughed. "Maybe I'm cooking supper tonight," Rachael teased.

"Then I'm sure it will be delicious, since your mother has probably taught you well."

Rachael scowled. "You're no fun. You're supposed to run for the hills, like a lonesome cowboy."

Bill laughed heartily. "I'm hardly a cowboy. I do like to eat though and I like all your company, so there, you can't scare me away."

Angel was happy to see her children having fun. She had not had a chance to speak further with Mae about the dancing, but she hoped it would pass and Mae would become more tolerant of Bill being around. The more he was around and the more good times they had would make things much easier on her. She sighed deeply and smiled secretly to herself. It was a good day.

Rachael looked up at her mother. "How are things going at the manor, Mom?"

"Very well. A lot has been done inside and I'm anxiously waiting for the weather to warm enough so they can get started on the old barn."

"What are they doing to the barn?"

"That's where the artists and writers will be working. I hope it'll be a very calm and peaceful place, and I'm planning to put in a waterfall to make it more relaxing there."

"Wow, Mom, you're going all out," Rachael remarked.

Bill had been watching Mae who had been sitting quietly. He

wondered what was going on in her young mind, and how she really felt about him. When Angel talked about the manor, Bill immediately thought of them moving there and wondered how the girls were taking the move.

"Rachael, you should see what your mother has done to the top level," he said. "You're really going to be impressed with that."

"What's going on with the top floor, Mom? Isn't it just more guest rooms?"

Angel had not yet told either Mae or Rachael about selling their current house. She had planned to do it later, but not while Bill was around. But now she was caught in a question that she had to answer.

"Oh, I've turned it into living quarters. It has an amazing kitchen and a whirlpool tub—"

"Who's it for?" Rachael looked mystified.

"For us…Mae and myself and of course you, when you're home."

"What?" Rachael's mouth dropped open, and Mae stared at her mother with wide eyes.

Bill winced as he took in their reaction. He wished he had kept his mouth shut and not got Angel into this predicament before she had been ready to tell the girls.

"What are you talking about?" Rachael sounded dumbfounded.

Angel's mouth opened; she searched for the right words. She knew she couldn't stop now, so she forged on trying to form some kind of meaningful words that would calm the girls. "Well, someone has to live there, Rachael, and I don't need two houses."

Rachael's face reddened and her fists balled up with white knuckles. She was half off her stool. "You're planning to sell our house?"

"That's right."

Rachael moved slowly and stood in front of Angel, displaying a confrontational stance. "What? You want to sell our house…this house…the house where I've lived all my life? You can't do that." She now had a finger under Angel's nose. "This is our home!"

Angel took a step backward, out of the line of Rachael's ferocity. "Rachael, calm down! I wanted to tell you before but the time was not right."

"Sure, Mom. You could have told me any number of times. How long have you been planning to do this? Since last fall?"

Angel wrung her hands. "I suppose."

"Then, why the big secret?" Rachael zoomed past Angel, leaving her mother standing in bewilderment.

Angel turned to Mae, who was now staring into her empty cup. "Well, what do you think, Mae? You might as well put your two cents worth in as well."

Bill felt that Angel was over the top and hardly knew what she was saying anymore. But he felt a need to keep quiet and keep out of this family dispute, even though he knew he had started it.

Mae looked up at Angel, her face screwed up and she jumped off the stool and ran to her mother and buried her head in her lap. She started to cry. Angel wrapped her arms around her baby. "It's going to be okay, Mae, you'll see."

Mae jerked her face up; tears were streaming down her cheeks. "That's what you always say. But it won't be okay." She pulled away and looked over at Bill. "And nothing's okay anymore. Why were you dancing with my mother last night? You're not my father. My father used to dance with my mother, and you can't!" She turned her face towards Angel. "And…and…I hate you. Just leave me alone." Mae bounded up the stairs, following in her older sister's footsteps.

Angel went limp and her shoulders slumped inward. She turned to Bill and all colour had drained from her face. "Look, I'm sorry. I didn't know they didn't know," Bill explained. Angel started to follow the girls up the stairs, but Bill laid a hand on her arm. "Maybe you should let them be for a bit. Let them think about it, they'll come around. And remember, Angel, it's your decision not the girls. You have to get on with your life and be strong."

"Save the lecture, Bill. Maybe you should just go."

"That's what you'd like wouldn't you? To just curl up and not face this?" He walked Angel into the living room, and sat her on the sofa. "This is your decision."

"If it's my decision, then why are you hanging around? You did enough damage today."

Her words hit Bill but he was determined to not abandon her now. She needed him, and by God he was going to show her that he could be counted on, despite his earlier foul-up.

Angel opened the patio door and stepped outside to get some air. Bill followed her and told her again that he was sorry. "I spoke when I shouldn't have, I know. And if you really want me to go, then I will. But damn it, Angel, if this is the way you handle things, then I'm not sure I want any part of it."

Angel acted like she didn't hear him talk. "I need to be alone with the girls right now. We have a lot to talk about."

Bill and Angel stepped back inside and she closed the patio door. He went directly to the foyer. As far as he was concerned, she had given him his answer. She wanted to be alone, and she didn't care what his opinion was. He was out of there.

As he grabbed his boots and jacket, he noticed one pair of boots was missing. They had all been lined up in a row and the smallest pair, Mae's, was no longer there. He looked up and called to Angel, "Where's Mae's boots?"

Angel walked to the door and scoured the area. She checked in the closet and said, "Her jacket's missing also."

Just then they heard a motor and a whine and Bill pulled the door open. He saw Mae streaking by on the snowmobile. "She's heading for the back," Bill told Angel, as he grabbed his coat and finished pulling on his boots. "Don't worry. Mae knows how to drive that thing." Bill hopped on his snowmobile and headed towards the back of the house as well and down the back snowmobile trail.

Angel walked the floor, her hand across her mouth. She hoped that Bill could catch up with Mae, but what would happen? Would Mae stop when she saw him behind her? Or would she try and go faster to get ahead of him? A picture of her baby girl turned upside down on a revving snowmobile flashed through her mind. She jumped when Rachael came down the stairs.

"What's going on? Where's Mae?"

Angel turned and ran to her daughter. "Oh, Rachael. Mae took off on the snowmobile, now Bill has gone after her."

"I thought it was just Bill leaving, then I heard another snowmobile start up. What's he going to do when he finds her? How's he going to get her to stop that thing?"

Angel could see how upset Rachael was, and despite her own beliefs she felt she had to calm her daughter.

"Don't worry, Rachael. Bill knows what he's doing, and he'll bring Mae back safe and sound." As she said the words, she hoped that was the way things would turn out.

****

Bill followed along the trail and as he rounded a curve, he saw Mae just ahead, and she was not going slowly. He was worried, hoping she was not so upset that she would lose control of the machine. He didn't know what he would do when he caught up with her, if he caught up with her, but he decided that staying a distance behind and not pursuing her too closely would probably be the best thing to do. He hoped that sooner or later she would stop and he could talk to her.

Another curve came along and when he rounded it, he didn't see Mae anymore. Just past the curve was another trail off to the left. He assumed that maybe she took that trail, in hopes of losing him. He turned down the trail and discovered it was not in as good a shape as the main road was. He bumped along realizing that the snow was soft there.

He was not on the trail long and was speeding along pretty good, because he wanted to get her in his view again, when the machine blunted into something and rose in the air, like it was taking off. Bill struggled to pull it down, but it tipped and fell sideways. He was thrown off and landed about ten feet from the machine. He jumped up to get back to the snowmobile, which was whirling and whining, but he was stopped by pain. His right leg gave out on him and when he leaned to stop a fall, he realized that his left shoulder was damaged as well.

Pain enveloped his body and he fell to the ground. After a minute he rose again, this time more carefully. He dragged himself towards the snowmobile, and managed to get it shut off then looked around, wondering what in the world he had hit.

He discovered it was a huge groundhog den. And because of the softening snow from the sunny day, it had been exposed and was sticking up. He shook his head wondering how Mae managed to miss it...if she was even on that trail. What a mess the day had turned into. He was not only incapacitated, but he also didn't even know now where Mae was.

If only he could get the snowmobile turned upright. He couldn't walk much, but he could drive it and head back to the house. It looked like he would need more help in finding Mae before darkness set in.

He tried to turn the machine but it was stuck, wedged in a snow bank, and he was in no condition to get it out. He collapsed on the ground with darkness not far away.

****

Back at the house, Angel and Rachael worried. Angel couldn't stop herself from walking the floor, and Rachael looked out the back window.

"I don't see anything. No lights and no snowmobiles. And it's getting dark."

Angel twisted her hands together and could only rely on Bill knowing how to get Mae back home.

"I can't stand it, Mom. I'm going back in the woods and look for them." Rachael rushed to the foyer with Angel behind her.

"Don't you think it's better if we wait here, Rachael?"

Rachael looked her mom in the eye and replied, "No!"

When she saw that she couldn't stop Rachael from going, Angel got her own gear on, and they both left the house and headed for the back trail.

****

Bill didn't know how long he had been lying on the ground drifting in and out of consciousness, because of the pain and cold. He hoped that another snowmobile would come along, as the trails were usually busy at night. He wondered where Mae had gone and thought that if she had not

124

taken that trail then maybe she had just gotten too far ahead of him for him to see. He thought maybe she might have gone over to the manor for some reason, or by now that she might have returned home.

If so, Angel would tell her that he had followed her and surely someone would come looking for him, perhaps Rachael on the snowmobile. That was all he could hope for as he lay in pain, having given up on any idea of being able to tip his snowmobile upright.

As he sat there on the ground, he heard a faint sound that grew closer. He looked up to see a snowmobile coming towards him. It was travelling very slowly and without headlights. The light was growing dim in the waning afternoon, and it took him some time to make out that it was Mae. He heaved a sigh of relief as she pulled up to him and stopped the machine.

"I don't know where the headlight switch is," she said.

Bill pulled himself up and hobbled over to the machine. He pulled the lights on and looked at her. "I've been hurt, Mae. You're going to have to take us back. I'm so glad you're okay."

Mae said nothing and Bill got himself on the back and told her to drive slowly.

"I've never driven at night before and I'm scared."

"Well, it's up to you to get us back now. I can't make it without you." Mae drew in a long breath and started the snowmobile. "Go carefully," he yelled, over the motor, "and watch the road. If you see any lumps go around them or stop. The ground is softer this time of year and you must be more careful. Okay, go. I think once you get off this trail it will be better on the big road. Head home."

****

Rachael ran down the trail and Angle had a hard time keeping up with her. "Mom," she called back, "why don't you just go back and wait."

But Angel wouldn't do that. Her little girl was out there somewhere on a snowmobile and it was almost dark. Rachael was at the top of the hill and Angel was at the bottom, when they saw a snowmobile coming over the hilltop. It was coming slowly and the lights were bright in their eyes.

Rachael moved to the side as did Angel. As it approached, Angel wasn't sure it was either Mae or Bill. It was hard to make out the snowmobile at this time of late day. But as it approached and stopped, Mae yelled, "Mommy." She jumped off and ran to her mother. "Mommy, I'm scared and I'm sorry."

Mae ran past Rachael and into her mother's arms. Rachael kept going towards the snowmobile. She got on it and started up the motor. She reached Mae and Angel and stopped, idling the motor. "I'll just keep going. I think he's hurt."

"What?" Angel shouted. She now realized that Bill was on the back of the machine. As Rachael rode onward, Angel asked, "What happened, Mae?"

Mae was sniffing and had to take a deep breath. "I went up a side trail and when I got so far it ended so I had to turn around. When I came back I saw him sitting on the ground."

"What?"

"His snowmobile was in the snow bank. Oh, Mommy, I didn't mean to cause all this trouble. Is he going to be okay?"

"I don't know, Mae. I don't know what's wrong with him." She and Mae hurried back to the house. When they got there, Bill and Rachael were sitting on the step.

"Mom," Rachael called. "Help me get him inside."

Angel and Rachael took each side of Bill and practically dragged him inside the house. When they got inside, Rachael attempted to take his jacket off, but he screamed when she tried to remove the sleeve on his left arm.

"Oh, oh, doesn't look good," Rachael said. "Might be broken." She put the jacket back on and said to her mother, "We've got to get him to emergency…now."

They all went to the car, Angel and Rachael dragging on Bill again. They got him in the back seat with Mae, and Rachael drove to the hospital.

At the hospital they took Bill right in, while Angel and the girls sat there waiting. All was quiet and Angel reached out and took both their hands in hers. As she sat with the girls, she thought of all that had taken place since last summer. The horrible moment when she had heard of Jake's death, the frightening scene when she'd gone to the manor after Arnold's frantic phone call about May, and the devastating moment when they could not revive her aunt's heart.

Now, after all this time, things had started to look better. Today had been a good day until now. Angel hoped that Bill's injuries were not life threatening, because she had no idea what was wrong with him except what Rachael had said about him maybe having a broken arm.

****

When Bill finally appeared, he was being pushed in a wheelchair by a nurse. He had been in there a long time. The nurse looked at Angel and the girls. "He has a badly sprained ankle and his shoulder was out of joint. The doc put it back and he's going to be okay. He has a bump on his head so he's going to have a bad headache for a bit."

Angel sighed with relief. The girls rose and Angel got behind the wheelchair. "Rachael, will you bring the car up to the door, please?" She turned to the nurse. "Are you sure he's okay to go home?"

"I'm okay to go home," Bill spoke up.

The nurse smiled. "He'll be fine, but he needs to keep quiet and off that ankle as much as possible."

Bill was woozy. They had given him something that hit him like a tractor trailer. He tried to stay awake but he kept drifting. He knew he was in a wheelchair and that was about it. He felt numb otherwise.

In the car he tried to talk when he was coherent. Mae had driven home in the front seat, while Angel had decided to sit in back with Bill. He looked over at Angel. "I don't think I can take the snowmobile home, tonight. Will you drive me?"

Angel looked horrified. "Drive you? You can't go home."

"But—"

"Forget it, Bill. You're going home with us."

"I have to go home, what about Ralph? He's probably doing a dog dance all over the kitchen by now."

Angel thought about the situation. "Rachael," she said. "Swing by the house so I can get a few things. I'm going home with Bill."

****

When they finally made it to the cabin and managed to drag Bill inside, they dropped him on the sofa in the living room. Angel turned to the girls. "You go home. I'll call you in the morning. Rachael, put the snowmobile inside and call Tanya. See if she knows anyone that can come over tomorrow and go back and get Bill's snowmobile out of the ditch."

"Okay, Mom." Rachael gave Angel a hug and Angel thought about the harsh words that were said earlier. They would have time later to talk about that.

Mae reached up and hugged her mother. "When are you coming home, Mommy?"

"I'll be home tomorrow. Rachael will have to come get me. I'll call you guys. Now go home and go to bed and don't worry."

CHAPTER SIXTEEN

After the girls left, the first thing Angel did was let Ralph outside. He had most certainly been doing the doggy dance, and Angel thought that if they'd been much longer there would have been a puddle in the middle of the kitchen, or somewhere. She watched him as she wasn't sure if he would go away or not. But Ralph did his business and ran straight back to the front door.

Angel let him in and he bounded over to Bill, his tail wiggling frantically behind him. "Ralph, you come here, right now," Angel commanded.

Ralph stopped in his tracks and looked at Angel. She motioned for him to come to her and he did. It seemed that Bill had been teaching him some manners. "You lie down now, right here in the kitchen…and stay!"

Ralph did as he was told although he whined a little bit. Angel walked to the sofa and saw that Bill had his eyes closed. He had only had his jacket draped around his shoulders so she tried to manoeuvre it off him. But Bill groaned so she thought it best to leave things as they were. She got his feet up on the sofa and made him as comfortable as she could. Then she decided to go to the bedroom and bring out the comforter. Bill was sleeping on the sofa tonight.

After she tucked him in, Angel took a seat in the leather recliner. The room was damp and cold and she decided it needed some heat. There was a pile of wood beside the Franklin stove and Angel decided to make a fire. If Bill woke up it would be warm and cozy in the room.

Once the fire got blazing well, Angel returned to the recliner. She sat and stared into the flames. She was tired. It had been a hard day. She knew the girls would be okay. She wondered what Tanya would do when she heard about all of this. She'd probably be over to Angel's house looking after the girls, when they were perfectly capable of looking after themselves. She hoped that Rachael wouldn't call Tanya that night. She had forgotten to tell her to wait until morning.

Angel felt hungry and decided to raid the fridge. She found eggs and ham inside but decided to leave that until morning. She reached in the cupboard and pulled out a box of corn flakes. She splashed milk on them and a dash of sugar and made a slice of toast.

She put the kettle on and made a pot of tea. On occasion she glanced into the living room to see if Bill had moved or not. He was like in the land of the dead. What ever kind of pain killer they had given him in the hospital it must have been strong.

After eating and cleaning up, Angel made a trip to the bathroom. She found some toothpaste and brushed her teeth. She hated going to bed without cleaning her teeth. She had brought along a nightdress and robe, so she changed in the bathroom.

She took her second cup of tea into the living room and stretched out on the recliner. While Angel had her eyes closed, Ralph sneaked into the living room and lay down beside her. She opened them with a start when she felt someone licking her hand that had dropped to the side of the recliner. She smiled as Ralph looked up at her with his big brown eyes.

"You go to sleep, mister." Angel stared into the flames that were waning now. She got up and found the thermostat, looked around and figured out that there were electric baseboards in the cabin. The temperature had been set at 12 degrees Celsius. Angel moved it up to 20. It was still cold outside and she didn't want Bill to be cold or herself.

She went back into the bedroom and found another comforter, which she brought out and placed over her after she'd lain back in the recliner. It was a soft, comfortable leather chair and Angel was warm and sleepy. She dozed off in the quiet of the cabin.

****

She awoke to the sound of scraping. When she opened her eyes, she saw Bill down on one knee, with his other leg with the cast stretched forward. "What in the world are you doing?"

Angel jumped up from the recliner. Bill looked up at her and smiled. "Trying to clean the stove."

"Well, here, give that shovel to me. You shouldn't be doing that."

"Hey, I'm not an invalid."

Angel gave him a look. "Really? You looked pretty bad off last night."

"Well, that was last night." Bill struggled to pull himself up by leaning on the arm of a chair.

"Really, Bill, why didn't you wake me up?"

"No need."

Angel shook her head and got down on her knees to finish the cleaning. She then proceeded to start a fire. Bill stood behind her leaning on a chair. "Go sit down," Angel ordered.

"You're pretty bossy for a guest."

Angel rephrased. "Please, sit down, Bill."

"I'm going to the kitchen to see what's for breakfast." He was leaning on a broom as he hobbled out of the living area.

"I'll get that. I already know what's for breakfast. But if you insist, I would like an egg and ham please, you can get started. I'll be there shortly."

After Angel had the fire going and the blue flames were licking at the kindling she had placed there, she went into the kitchen.

"Easy to tell you're a mother."

Angel grinned. "Bill, you really need to take it easy. How's that lump on your head?" She moved in front of his chair and touched the top of his forehead that had been covered with a wide bandage.

Bill reached up and slid his arms around her waist. He pulled her down on the chair and kissed her. "Now, that's a proper good morning."

Angel jumped up and brushed her hair back from her face. "Bill, you could have hurt yourself. I'm heavy."

He laughed loudly. "For fuck's sake I told you I'm not an invalid. I've got a bump on the head, a sore shoulder and a sprained ankle. I'm not dying. Did you enjoy the kiss?"

"Bill, you're teasing me."

"I don't mean to. If I was in better shape I would want to do more than kiss you, now that I have you all to myself."

Angel didn't reply. She opened the fridge door, pulled out the ham and went to the cupboard to open the eggs that Bill had retrieved earlier. She opened a bottom cupboard door and pulled out a large frying pan.

Bill was observing her. "Well, you seem to know your way around my kitchen."

"I was here before, remember? I made rice."

"Oh, yeah." Bill got up, still relying on the broom for a homemade crutch. "Least I can do is put the coffee on."

When the eggs and ham were cooked and the coffee was ready, they sat and had breakfast. Bill had calmed down and Angel noticed he had gone quiet. She thought back to her earlier diagnosis of him that he might be bi-polar then she dismissed the thought. He was probably just feeling sicker than he had let on. She had seen him reach up a couple of times and rub the spot where the head wound was.

When they had finished, Angel volunteered to clean up the kitchen. Bill did not disagree. Instead he went to his bedroom, then the bathroom. When he returned with clean clothing on, Angel had dressed and was back in the living room adding wood to the fire.

"I wonder how my snowmobile is," Bill said.

"Oh, I asked Rachael to call around and see if she could find someone to bring it out of the woods for us."

"Thanks," Bill said, and shuffled over to the sofa and plunked himself down, stretching the injured leg out in front of him.

Angel got up from the fire. "I'm going to call Rachael now and get her to come get me. I'll be back later tonight to see if you need anything done."

"No need, Angel. I can look after myself from here on out. You need to go home and be with the girls. Isn't Rachael leaving today?" Seeing that Angel was looking reluctant, he continued, "I called my brother this morning and he's coming out to stay with me for a bit."

"Oh, that's good. I wouldn't want to think of you being here alone in your condition."

Bill gave her a sarcastic grin. "Yes, mother hen." Then his face took on a more serious look. "I'm sorry about yesterday. If I hadn't opened my big mouth about the manor, none of this would have happened. And I wouldn't have ruined your weekend with Rachael."

"Really, Bill, I should have told them before. Rachael had every right to be upset. I mean she was shocked, you could tell that."

"Yes, she was shocked all right, and pretty damn mad at you. I hope you can smooth things over."

"Of course we can. I'm going to have a talk with them as soon as I get home. And don't go blaming yourself. I said a couple of mean things to you and I'm sorry as well."

"Forget it," Bill said. "I hope you won't mind my snowmobile hanging around your yard for a bit, if you do find someone to dig it out of the ditch. I'll send my brother down if you can't find anyone."

Angel called Rachael, and before long the girls arrived and Angel left the cabin as soon as they drove in the yard. Bill sat on a kitchen chair and watched her go. "Good bye, Angel," he said to the closed door. "Have a great life."

****

After Angel and the girls arrived home, Angel told them she wanted to have a talk. She gathered her girls in the living room and as they sat looking at her she said, "Yesterday was not a good day, part of it was, but the rest fell apart. I'm sorry, Rachael that your weekend was so messed up—"

"Mom—"

"Let me finish then you can say whatever you want to say after, okay?"

The girls kept quiet and Angel continued to talk. "In the first place, I shouldn't have been so secretive about selling the house. But I knew what a blow it was going to be to both of you. I do know how much this house means to you girls. It means everything to me as well. But as you look at it as the place you grew up and as your home, I look at it differently.

"I cherish my years here with your father and when you guys were little kids. I will remember them fondly forever. But I just don't want to live here anymore. There are too many memories here of your father. Every time I go up to my bedroom I think of him and wish he were there with me. I need a clean break from this place. I know you probably don't understand, Mae, but I was hoping you would, Rachael."

Rachael got up and walked over to her mother. She leaned down and hugged her. "Since you put it that way, Mom, I'm beginning to see your side of things." She sat beside her mother, and Mae joined them.

"I know it's going to be hard, girls. Mae what do you have to say?"

Mae was silent and just hunched her shoulders.

Angel encouraged Mae to sit between herself and Rachael. She put an arm around her youngest daughter, and thought about what Bill had said to her. *You have to be strong, Angel, it's your life.* "Mae, we won't be moving for a few months yet. So you'll have time to get used to the idea. And although we didn't get to the manor this time when Rachael was home, maybe you and I could have a look at your bedroom sometime soon over there and you could tell me what colour you'd like to paint it."

"Can it be purple?" Mae spoke up, seemingly in a brighter mood.

Angel laughed. "It can be any colour you want it to be. It's your bedroom. And you can decorate it anyway you want. Rachael, if you have any ideas about what you might want, you can phone or text me with your ideas. Otherwise I'll wait until you get home at Easter."

"I'd rather you wait, Mom. I need to have a look at the place before I can decide."

Angel thought things were going pretty well, and after supper when Rachael was about to leave, she told her mom that she was sorry for getting angry at her. She also told her that she had a talk with Mae about Bill and hoped it might help some.

"I'm happy for you and Bill, and I think that if you really care for each other then you should go for it."

Angel hugged Rachael. "How did you get so wise, for such a young woman?"

Rachael hugged Mae and said, "Take it easy on our mom. She's doing the best she can."

After Rachael had gone and Angel had tided up the kitchen, she went into the family room to see Mae. "You got a minute?"

Mae was watching TV. "Sure. That program's boring anyway."

Angel sat down. "So, care to tell me about the talk you and Rachael had?"

"About you?"

"Well, yes, me and I guess Bill also."

"She just told me about when she was little and when she met you. She told me that she was glad that Dad had gotten married again, and that it was what people did sometimes when someone died."

"Life goes on, Mae. Even though we are sad. Other people sometimes come into our lives and make us feel happy."

"Does he make you feel happy?"

"Sometimes. And I'm happy when we're all together doing fun things."

"Like we used to do with Daddy?"

"Yes, like that."

"I guess he's okay. I like his house, and I like Ralph. I like that he takes me on the snowmobile and fishing. Do you think we might all go out on the boat someday?"

"You mean, Bill's boat, to fish?"

"No, I mean the sailboat, Daddy's sailboat."

"Oh, I don't know about that, Mae. I don't know if Bill can sail. I'd have to talk to him about it."

"We can teach him. Rachael and me."

Angel smiled. "Well, we'll ask him. Okay?"

Mae got up and hugged her mom. "Okay. I should go up and get my stuff ready for school tomorrow."

When Mae left the room, Angel shut off the TV. She decided to call Bill and see how he was doing.

****

April came in with warmer weather, and the snow started disappearing. Bill's brother had come to take the snowmobile home, and one of Bill's neighbours had driven him down. Bill was keeping close to the cabin, and Angel hadn't seen him since the accident.

Angel was pleased as to how things were coming along at the manor, and she knew that it wouldn't be long before the workers would be outside converting the old barn into a writer's and painter's work area. Excited about the possibilities of it all, she wished she could share her excitement with Bill, but since the snowmobile accident, he had not visited. Of course she understood that he could not travel for a while, but it had been three weeks, and although she'd called him a few times, he seemed distant and didn't stay on the phone long. He always had an excuse it seemed to Angel, always something he had to attend to in order to get off the phone.

Easter was approaching and Rachael would soon be home. Angel contemplated calling Bill and inviting him for Easter dinner. She had already made arrangements with Tanya and Bob to come over. She had hoped that he would call her, but that did not happen, and Angel had her pride. She felt that if he did not call her, she was not going to make a nuisance of herself by calling him all the time.

She felt that Bill might have had a change of heart concerning her, and maybe she should try and move on also. But she was finding that very difficult to do, and she wished for the return of the earlier days, when she could always run stuff by him and get his input into the operation of the retreat.

****

133

Bill Canton stretched and flexed his ankle. It was feeling good and he was glad the cast was finally off. His shoulder didn't hurt anymore and the bump on his head had gone away also, taking along with it those excruciating headaches.

Another headache that had just walked out the door a few days ago, was his brother, Eric. After he'd told Angel a white lie about calling his brother to come visit, Bill had actually done it. Although he had told Angel that day she left his place that he was feeling fine and his brother was coming, it was all a pack of lies. In fact, he had been feeling shitty that morning.

What he remembered clearly though was pulling Angel down on his knee despite the pain and kissing her. What he remembered more clearly was Angel jumping up and ignoring his remark that he would like to do something more than kiss her, if he was feeling better. So, it left a bad taste in Bill's mouth.

Things were not going well between them. If he was going to make a long term commitment to anyone, he wanted the other person to do the same. And it seemed to him that Angel Jordan was a bit wishy-washy in that department. Besides, all that trouble with her girls...not Rachael, but the other one in particular, was a little too much for him.

He closed his eyes and thought about that beautiful red hair, those striking blue eyes, and a body that looked like she'd never had a kid. But what he loved most about Angel was her smile, and the way she laughed when she was relaxed enough to do so.

Bill got up to try out his ankle and it felt like it was good as new. The last time he'd had an accident, he had similar injuries, but it was the other leg and arm. It was the same head though, and the headaches he had were similar enough to the ones he'd had after the car accident. He hoped he wouldn't have any more accidents any time soon. He was running out of legs and arms and heads.

He walked in the living room to tend the fire. It had been a nice warm day but the evenings were still chilly, so he started up a fire and stood watching the kindling crackling. It bothered him to not be in touch with Angel, and she'd called him a number of times to see how he was doing. It had been awhile now since she'd called. He figured she was either mad at him or waiting for him to call her. He knew he should, and he knew he should explain things, but he couldn't do it.

For one thing, as soon as she turned those baby blues on him, he would be a piece of mush all over again. Bill always considered himself a tough guy. Even when Lorraine had left him, he didn't take that long to get over her. But, the circumstances had been different. Lorraine had left him for his buddy. Now that made him mad and it was far easier to get over than Angel was going to be.

The trouble with Angel was that she didn't even realize how much he cared for her. It was obvious from the way she acted when she was last at the cabin. She treated him like a patient. Like maybe how she might treat her kids or her students when she was a teacher.

Bill sighed and added a couple of logs to the fire. He had to stop thinking like this. He'd as much as made up his mind that he and Angel were over, if there ever was anything between them in the first place.

CHAPTER SEVENTEEN

Sunny days and warm temperatures finally came to the Valley, and the snow was replaced with shootings of green grass, lilies, crocuses and daffodils. The snowmobile days were over for the season and the cover had been placed back over the machine until next winter. Angel had decided to sell the newer snowmobile and had no trouble doing so. That money could easily be used towards the conversion taking place in the old barn.

Mae was doing well in school and she even on occasion had asked Angel about Bill. She was wondering why he hadn't been around. Angel told her that Bill was busy on some project, which was an excuse but as far as Angel knew it could have been true. Angel put her energy into looking after Mae, occasionally dropping by to see Tanya and Bob, and moving headlong into the retreat renovations.

On a sunny day just before Easter, Arnold Brooks dropped by. When Angel went to the door, he was standing there holding something.

"Hi, Arnold, long time no see. How are you?"

"Dandy. I've got something for you, Angel."

Angel took the envelope that he shoved under her nose. "Why, Arnold, why don't you come in and have some tea with me?"

Arnold followed Angel into the foyer and slipped his shoes off at the door.

"Come right in the living room. I'm anxious to see what you brought me." Angel slipped the pages out of the envelope and skimmed them. "Why, Arnold, this is most fascinating. I never realized there was so much history behind that old manor. I had thought that my uncle had built it. Now you tell me that it belonged to an old sea captain who built it for his wife. Later she died in childbirth, poor thing. I'm dying to read the rest of this, but not right now." Angel laid the pages on the coffee table and went to the kitchen. She returned with a plate of oatmeal cookies and a pot of tea. "I know these won't be as good as Aunt May's, but Arnold, I try."

Arnold scoffed and rubbed the top of his bald head. "Oh now, Angel, May always told me that you were a good cook. She said she couldn't tell the difference between her cookies and the ones you made."

Angel laughed. "That's nice of you to say, Arnold. So you've been keeping well?"

"I have. But I'm givin' up my house. My daughter wants me to move in with her. And I guess she's right. Last winter was a long and hard one. I 'bout froze in that big house. Gonna put a for sale sign on it this week. Tell me about the manor and how it's comin' along. I went by there the other day, and there were cars and trucks lined up and so much goin' on there

136

that I thought if May was here she'd be puttin' the boot to all of them." Arnold laughed heartily.

"Well, I'm sorry to hear that you're leaving your house, Arnold. But I'm sure you'll enjoy it at your daughter's. You two were always really close, weren't you?"

"Oh, yes. She's so much like her dear mother." Arnold rubbed at his eyes. "I miss her you know, Angel. I miss her a lot...and May too." His eyes got bright and a smile crossed his face. "I'm tellin' you, when the three of us got together it was a grand time. May never could keep her opinions to herself, and she sure loved to beat me at any game we had. Mabel never cared for games. She would sit and knit and watch us play. I think she got a kick out of listenin' to us banter back and forth."

Angel smiled. "I'm sure she did. And I'm sure that this info you brought me is going to be very helpful. Thank you, Arnold, for taking the time to write all this for me."

Arnold placed his teacup on the coffee table and got up. "It was a pleasure. I hope it comes in handy. Now I have to get goin'. So much to do before I get that for sale sign on the lawn." He shook his head. "It's hard, Angel, but I know it's the right thing to do."

Angel gave Arnold a hug and he pulled his shoes on and waved her a goodbye, as he went strolling down the lane.

Easter was a family affair. Rachael arrived home on Friday and the three of them went over to the manor on Saturday to look at the top floor. The girls were anxious to talk about their bedrooms.

Mae was holding a purple paint chip out to Rachael. "Look, Rachael, this is the colour of my bedroom. I can't wait to see it all finished."

Rachael laughed. "Well, one thing I can say, it's bright!"

"Have you decided what colour you want your bedroom?"

"No," Rachael replied. "I've got a few ideas, but now that I've seen the room I think it might be either, beige or blue."

"What colour blue? Light or dark?"

"A nice light blue, like the sky."

"Rachael, you're boring." Mae laughed.

"I guess Rachael and you are not much alike when it comes to colour choices, but it will be fun to decorate the rooms. Now what colour do you think mine should be?" Angel asked.

"May looked thoughtful. "Hmmm, white?"

Angel laughed. "Well, that's kind of boring isn't it?"

"But you wear white almost all the time, Mom," Mae remarked.

Angel smiled at her. "I do like white, you're right. But I think I'll get a bit more creative with my bedroom. It will be a surprise, so you girls just wait."

Easter turned out to be a nice family time with Bob and Tanya, and on

Monday afternoon, Rachael packed up her car and headed back to Truro She hugged her mother and sister. "Next time I drive up that yard, I'll be here for the whole summer."

"Yay," Mae yelled.

Angel and Mae watched Rachael disappear down the driveway. Angel wiped a tear from her eye and put an arm around her youngest daughter. They walked back to the house.

****

May was turning into a busy month. Angel had drawn some sketches for the interior of the old barn and passed them on to the workers. She was pleasantly surprised when she visited to see that it had almost been completed.

"Wow, that's all I can say." Angel smiled at the workers that were putting on finishing touches. The waterfall at the end of the building looked soothing and relaxing. Upstairs in the loft there were individual cubicles for writers, who might prefer to work inside if the weather should not be to their liking. Downstairs was one open area where artists could work wherever they chose. The décor was old style, the old barn beams had been varnished a dark mahogany, and in between each beam was drywall, painted a lustrous white.

Angel thought the old building looked much higher than it had looked originally. The walls were painted individual colours, but all bright. One area had a golden yellow, and down from that was a rose so beautifully optimistic, that no artist would ever feel melancholy around it. Having different shades of colours over the walls was Angel's idea in order to bring balance and clarity to one's inventive thoughts. Now all the manor needed was guests.

Angel was looking into that. She already had a number of guests booked for the opening weekend, which would happen during the apple blossom festivities at the end of May. Many of the town's people and a few dignitaries would be on hand to help open the retreat. After she added photos of the interior of the old barn to her website, she imagined she would get a good response.

Because she had not heard from Bill, and because she had too much pride to call him, she hired someone to help set up her website. She had it pretty well worked out in her mind and just needed that extra web-design expertise to pull it all together. She was proud of the website and proud of what had become Angel's Retreat. The house was beautiful and held just the right amount of serenity that she'd been looking for.

Angle had to admit she was tired, and she was looking forward to Rachael coming home and giving her a hand with final touches. Mae had also been a great help once she decided that the manor wouldn't be such a bad place to live after all. Angel was very impressed with Mae's input for colour design at the manor. All in all, Angel had to admit that she even impressed herself. She just hoped that these first guests would enjoy their stay and pass on their experience to others.

****

Rachael's employment at the clinic for the summer was not to start until the first of June. She was happy about that because she knew her mother needed help. She just wished that things had not gone so bad between her mother and Bill Canton. She had asked about him a few times when she'd called her mother, but her mother was always evasive. Rachael didn't know what had really happened between them, but she promised herself that she would find out when she got home.

Everything looked so different driving up the lane. The grass was green; flowers were poking out here and there and Rachael was glad to be home. Then a melancholy feeling hit her. It wouldn't be long before she would not be driving up this lane to the house that had been her childhood home. She thought about the cubby hole and decided that who ever moved there might have kids who would definitely enjoy it. She was grown up now, and she didn't need it anymore.

Rachael shook off the feeling because she wanted things to be good between her and her mother. She knew that this move was the right thing for Angel, and now that Bill was not in the picture, her mother would need the manor all the more, in order to keep her going. But, if she had anything to do with it, she was going to get to the bottom of this breakup between her mother and Bill. The two of them had just been too happy together, and Rachael couldn't see how things could have fallen apart so quickly.

She opened the door and called, "Mom, you home?" The house was quiet. Rachael dragged her bags inside and went out for more stuff. After she had it all in the foyer, she dragged it all upstairs to her bedroom. Still no one was around. Rachael decided she knew where they might be and got in her car and drove to the manor. What she found there was a beehive of activity, and her mother was in the middle of it. Poor Mom, she thought, she really needs help.

"Hey, Mom, got a hug for your daughter?"

Angel reeled around then made straight for Rachael. "Rachael, I didn't expect you until tomorrow."

Angel gave Rachael a big hug and Rachael replied, "Well, I'm full of surprises you know. I just couldn't wait to get home."

"Boy, am I glad you're here. I've got about a million jobs for you, don't worry, most of them aren't hard work. You're going to be my go-getter girl."

Rachael laughed. "And what exactly does that mean?"

"I've got so many things that need attending to, and I can't get away from this place to do them. You wouldn't believe what a big help your little sister has been. And even Tanya's been over here…like she has time."

Rachael was happy to see her mother beaming. "Give me the list and I'll get started. By the way, where's Mae?"

Angel looked around. "I really don't know, I guess you'll have to go look for her."

Rachael was impressed with the state of the manor. She had yet to see the old barn but first she wanted to find Mae. There were still workers everywhere, and Rachael decided to try the upper floor where they would be living. She was on the second floor when she heard Mae call her name.

"Hey, you're home. Isn't this place crazy?"

Rachael gave Mae a hug. "It's hectic all right. You busy?"

Mae shrugged. "Not really."

"Wanna come with me?"

"Where?"

"Wherever Mom has put on this list. I haven't looked at it yet, but I want to talk to you, so let's go."

In the car, Rachael checked the list. "Okay, we're going to the printers and pick up some business cards and brochures."

"What do you want to talk about?"

"This list isn't that long, but let's get out of here first." Rachael drove downtown and told Mae to wait in the car. When she came out, she turned to Mae. "Okay, tell me what's going on between Mom and Bill Canton."

Mae looked puzzled and blinked her eyes. "There's nothing going on. What do you mean? As far as I know Mom has not seen him. He's never been at the house lately."

"So Mom didn't tell you anything?"

"She told me he was working on some project and was busy."

"Hmmm. Okay, I guess I'll have to have a talk with Mom then."

"Why do you want to know?"

"Because she likes him, Mae, and he likes her."

Mae said nothing and Rachael continued on with the next thing on the list. She knew one thing; she was determined to find out why Bill was not around anymore. Maybe he did have a big project. If her mother couldn't tell her something satisfactory, Rachael would just have to go to the horse's mouth to find out.

****

That night when Angel got home from the manor and Rachael and

Mae got home from town, Rachael confronted her mother. They had all just finished up supper and Angel was looking at her website. Rachael walked in the living room and looked over her shoulder.

"Nice website, Mom. Bill help you with that?"

"Actually, no. I hired a web designer to get me going. Now I'm doing pretty good on my own."

"You're doing pretty good? What would make it better?"

Angel shut her laptop and turned around to look at Rachael. "What are you talking about?"

Rachael took a seat across from her mother. "Well, you said you were doing pretty good on your own, is that true?"

"Rachael, what's this all about?"

"It's about you and Bill. Can you explain to me why he isn't hanging around here or at the manor anymore? Every time I bring him up, you don't seem to want to talk about him."

"That's probably because there's nothing to talk about."

"So what happened?"

"Nothing happened."

"Mom. You're being evasive again."

Angel sighed and knew she wasn't going to get out of this as easily as she had been able to, while talking to Rachael on the phone. "The last time I saw him was the day you picked me up after the accident. I called him a few times and he was abrupt, always had something he had to attend to. After a bit I decided not to call anymore. I assumed that he didn't want to hear from me."

"And that's it?"

"Pretty much."

"You guys never even discussed anything?"

"I asked him how he was when I called and he said he was doing fine. And he asked me how I was doing, and I said I was busy but things were going well. Stuff like that."

"So you skirted around the problem and never got anywhere."

"Rachael, I didn't know what to say."

"Ahh, maybe, what's wrong Bill? Why haven't I seen you or heard from you, unless I call you?"

"After I'd called a few times to inquire about how he was doing, I assumed he was okay. He said his brother was there for a while, but that he was doing okay on his own by then, then he made some excuse about having to get off the phone. So one day I just decided to not call him again. I really did think that he would call me, but he hasn't."

"So you're just going to leave things like that…forever?"

Angel got up, she'd had enough of this and she was too tired and too busy to talk about William Canton. "I think he's bipolar. He's probably in his down time, depressed or whatever. I haven't time for someone like that. I've way too much to do."

Rachael got up. "Okay, Mom. Thanks for telling me, and I'm sorry things worked out this way."

Angel couldn't help it when tears formed in her eyes and she turned from Rachael, but it was too late, Rachael had seen them.

"Mom, why are you crying? You love him, don't you?"

"Stop it! It doesn't matter." Angel's tears were streaming now. "He wasn't what I thought he was. There'll never be anyone like your father. He was a good man, and I loved him. I thought that I could depend on Bill, but I was wrong."

Angel hadn't wanted this to happen, hadn't even expected that it would. She didn't even know where all the emotion had come from. She realized that all this time she hadn't been facing up to her true feelings. But what good did it do to let go? It wasn't going to fix things, and she had a big event ahead of her, she had to be strong. Be strong, Angel. This is your life. Isn't that what Bill had told her? Well, he got that right. She would be strong, no more emotional outbursts. She hoped that Rachael would leave her alone about it after this.

Angel dabbed at her eyes and composed herself. "Well, you found out what you wanted to know, whatever good it's going to do you, Rachael. But now that you know, let's get on with our lives. I'm okay."

Rachael hugged her mother. "I'll do whatever I can, Mom. Did I clear up a few errands for you today?"

Angel gave her a smile. "Yes, and thank you. But don't worry, by tomorrow there'll be another list."

Rachael told Angel that she was going out for a while to visit some friends. Angel was actually relieved. She needed some time alone to get herself together. A nice bubble bath would work.

The next day was another hectic one, but with Mae and Rachael's help, Angel got through it, and through the next couple of weeks. Things were all coming together, but Angel was nervous. Her guests would be arriving soon, and the big event was just a week away.

****

Rachael got up early. She wanted to get started on this day as she had a mission to accomplish. She heard her mother down in the kitchen so she went down to have breakfast. On her way past Mae's bedroom she looked in to see Mae still in bed.

"Get up, sleepy head. I want to talk to you later, and I want you to go with me on errands today."

Mae groaned, but pushed the blankets back. "Why do I have to go?"

"You'll see soon enough. What we do today is going to be important and I need your help."

Mae was now curious. "What are we doing?"

"Get up, get dressed and don't say a word about this to Mom." Rachael left Mae gaping at her and went downstairs. She found her mother sitting at the kitchen island drinking coffee and going over some papers. "Hey, Mom, whatcha got for me to do today?"

"I'm just now making a list."

Rachael went for the coffee. "Good, because I'm all rested up and ready to go."

"That's encouraging." Angel got up, passed a sheet of paper to Rachael, gave her a kiss on the cheek and said, "I'm off to the manor. Are you taking Mae with you?"

"Yes. She's getting dressed now."

After Angel left, Rachael scanned the list. It didn't look too long and she figured since it was early, she could get these things out of the way by at least eleven. She called upstairs, "Mae, you coming?"

Rachael and Mae had breakfast then they headed out. In the car Rachael told Mae her plan. "So I figure after we get these errands done, we can go to the lake and see Bill. Are you okay with this?"

"What are we doing that for?"

"Well, we need to talk to him. You do want Mom to be happy, don't you?"

"Yes."

"Well, she isn't happy now. She likes Bill and he likes her, so I want to find out what's going on."

"I like him too."

"You do? So do I. I think he's fun and I think he's good for our mother. She's lonely, Mae, and she misses Dad a lot."

"We had fun fishing."

"I heard about that. I'm glad you did."

The girls did the errands up with Mae mostly waiting in the car, while Rachael went from place to place. When Rachael returned from her last errand, she tossed the list in the back seat and looked over at Mae. "Okay, we're done. Let's go."

They drove to the lake and when they reached the cabin they saw Bill's car in the yard. Mae and Rachael got out of their car and approached the veranda. When Rachael knocked on the door, a dog barked. "That's Ralph," Mae said.

The door opened and Bill stood staring at the girls with a look of total surprise on his face. "Well, what are you two doing here? Is something wrong? Is your mother okay?"

Rachael stood staunchly. "Do you care?"

"Of course I care. What kind of question is that?"

He motioned for them to come inside, and Rachael wasted no time with the questions. "We're here for answers, Bill. Why have you stopped seeing my mother?"

Bill took a step back, as Rachael entered the cabin like a gust of strong wind. "You don't beat around the bush, do you?"

Mae rushed over to see Ralph and sat on the floor to play with him, while Rachael grabbed a kitchen chair and pulled it from the table. She sat down and Bill took another chair and joined her.

"I thought it was the best thing to do," Bill explained. "If I had tried to tell your mother that, she would only have tried to convince me that it wasn't. I didn't want to cause her any more anguish and family trouble."

"But you did cause her anguish," Rachael pointed out.

"Mom is sad a lot and I know she's thinking about you," Mae added. "But whenever I asked where you were, she said you were busy on a project."

Bill rubbed his head. "I'm sorry, girls. I…I don't know what to say. I'm just sort of shocked that you're here. I'm sorry I didn't discuss things more with your mother, but it's too late now. She has every right to be upset with me…forever."

"I don't think you're right, Bill," Rachael said. "I think you're being a coward. Running away from things. The least you could have done was discuss matters with her. She hasn't a clue what came over you. She said she thought you were bipolar."

"Yeah, she told me that before. Let me assure you I am not bipolar. I've caused a lot of family strain between you guys, and I thought my exit would be the best thing."

"So you thought that not explaining anything to Mom, just walking away and ignoring the whole situation, was the best thing to do?"

Bill got up and walked the floor. "I know what you're saying and you're right. But I don't know how to right the wrong."

"It's easy. Come to the retreat opening and support her. She's been doing everything herself. Now that I'm home, Mae and I are trying to help her, but what she needs is what only you can give her. That would make her happy."

"And what is that, Rachael?"

Rachael looked him in the eye. "Do you love her?"

"Like I said, you don't beat around the bush, do you?"

"Well, *you* are right now."

"What if your mother rejects me?"

"You're just being a coward again, and if she does, so what? You won't be any worse off than you are now. That is if you care about her."

"You've got a good point, and I do care about your mother. If I hadn't

I wouldn't have walked away."

Rachael rolled her eyes. "That's just stupid."

"Rachael, I know you girls are trying to be helpful, and I appreciate your input, but what goes on between your mother and me, should be between your mother and me."

"Then make it between you guys and we won't have to interfere. Right now we're just trying to help."

"Okay, I get you." Bill sat down again. "So you want me to just show up at the opening. It might be the worst thing I could do for your mother. If she has everything under control now, it might just upset her. I don't want to ruin her day."

Rachael got up. "Bill, you're impossible to talk to. I'm sorry I came. I can see you've got your mind made up, and I guess maybe Mom is better off without you. Come on, Mae."

The girls hurried out the door and Bill didn't try to stop them. He was sorry things worked out like they did, but this family was apparently tight knit and there didn't seem to be a place for him to fit in. His head was aching again and the dog was scratching at the door. Some days he thought it was better to not get out of bed.

CHAPTER EIGHTEEN

Angel awoke to a streaming sun blaring through the patio doors in her bedroom. She rose and opened the doors, stepped out on the balcony and gazed down on the sparkling pool below.

It was going to be one terrifically busy day. She wasn't thinking much of Bill these days. She was glad he had been there to help her get started, when she needed someone in her time of doom and gloom, but she was looking forward to the future and her new endeavour.

The way they had met could only have come to this. They had started a friendship based on how they each knew and cared about Jake. It was not a bad thing, but probably not a good basis for a new relationship.

Angel dressed hurriedly and bounced down the stairs to the kitchen. She had a quick breakfast of cereal and toast, juice and coffee. She didn't have the appetite or time for anything else. Just as she was stashing away her breakfast dishes and thinking of calling the girls, the doorbell rang.

A delivery truck stood in the driveway, and the driver was at her door holding a long box. Angel took it and laid it down. She went to the kitchen, returned and gave him a tip. As the truck rumbled down her driveway, Angel closed the door and picked up the box. When she lifted the lid it was what she had expected. More flowers. They had been coming since yesterday, and Angel was stacking her car to take them all over to the manor. But when she read the card, she decided these flowers would stay at her house. *Congratulations, Angel, in completing your dream. I wish you all the luck in the world. You are amazing. Bill.*

Angel was thunderstruck. After all this time he finally had made a connection. She thought of calling him but then things started happening. Her phone rang and then rang again. There were people waiting for her at the manor, and she had better get going.

She called upstairs to the girls. "Mae, Rachael, get up now. I have to leave for the manor. Come over after you have breakfast. Do you hear me?"

"Yes, Mom," Rachael called down the stairs. "I'm up and I'll go wake Mae. See you in a bit."

At the manor, Angel got busy with arranging and organizing everything, and thoughts of Bill were pushed back in her mind. She told herself on the way over to the manor, that when this day was over and things calmed down she should call him and thank him for the lovely flowers. But, she wasn't sure it would be appropriate, considering how they had left things. Perhaps it would be better if she just took that note as a goodbye.

Some of the guests that had booked the weekend were already at the manor. A couple of others were expected soon. News reporters with cameras were poking into her face, guests were milling about looking lost. Angel shooed the reporters out of the way and tended to her guests.

"Welcome to Angel's Retreat. I'm Angel Jordan. I hope you all will totally enjoy your time here and get your creative juices flowing also."

The guests smiled and nodded.

"Please, feel free to ramble around inside the manor and out into the old barn retreat. Take a walk in the orchard if you wish, it's beautiful down there now, all the apple blossoms are in full bloom."

Angel made her getaway outside to look for someone she knew. She saw Mae and Rachael just getting out of Rachael's car, and headed straight for them. She was going to need a little backup as this thing was starting to overwhelm her.

****

For the guests that entered through the doors, the first thing they saw was an attractive plaque containing the history of the manor. Mae and Angel both had a hand in the creative side of it, with Arnold's help in the wording, and it all came together with the help of a plaque maker.

The second thing they saw was a long, wide hallway with a door to the right leading into a dazzling white kitchen. Very modern in its layout, the kitchen offered guests an opportunity to prepare their own meals or have group cooking. The French doors were flung wide open and led guests into the welcoming dining area. A lovely chandelier hung from the centre of the room, which was decorated with maroon walls and all white, woodwork. Five roomy tables filled the room.

Back out in the hallway and across from the kitchen was a doorway leading to the Victorian living room. The furniture was dated but in good shape. A comfy sofa and soft, comfortable armchairs adorned the room. The fireplace at the end was a cozy addition for those cool and rainy days. One wall held stacks of worn books that looked like they had been loved and read many times.

When the guests returned to the hallway and walked farther down, they passed a door that was closed and marked *Private*. Unbeknownst to the guests this was Angel's office, den, and guest bedroom, or whatever else she wanted it to be. It had been the bedroom that May had occupied during the time she had broken her leg and was confined to the downstairs area.

Looking up, guests marvelled at the long, eloquent stairway, with hand crafted newel post and railings, all in a deep mahogany wood shade. As they ascended the stairs and reached the second level, they were welcomed by an even wider hallway with more armchairs, lamps and reading material.

Five themed bedrooms gave guests a chance to imagine what it was like to live in the olden days. There was the *Bay of Fundy Room*, with its four-poster bed covered in an off-white satin brocade; the *Apple Blossom Room*, with deep pinkish walls adorned with framed Victorian prints, and an old apple ladder in the corner of the room; the *Grandmother's Room*, with the cabaret-style lamps and the antique chaise lounge; the *Evangeline Room* depicting the lives of the early Acadians, featuring an antique quilt on the log bed, rustic nightstands and dresser, and a faux bear skin rug on the floor; and last but not least was the *Victorian Gardens Room*, which was the largest and most elaborate. Purples and reds adorned the room, a large round ornate mirror hung on one wall, and an antique brass chandelier dropped down from the ceiling. Posh velvet drapes hung from the windows, and of course all rooms were equipped with full, modern en-suites.

At the far end of the hallway was another guest sitting room. More chairs, books, and games, along with a huge TV, filled the room. Returning to the hallway, guests were stopped from climbing the third set of stairs, which were cordoned off with another *Private* sign. It was time for the guests to make their way outside and walk through the grounds or visit the old barn loft, where they would be greeted by the writers' cubicles, and also a closed off room that when opened revealed a large hot tub surrounded by exotic plants.

In the lower level of the old barn, the guests could ramble about and watch any of the painters that had begun a project. They could decide to take up a corner for themselves if they were a staying guest, or to wait until after the ceremony had finished and things calmed down somewhat.

****

It was high noon and all the chairs had been set up for the speaking guests, and other dignitaries. The podium was in place and a ribbon flapped in the wind waiting to be cut by Angel.

It was time for the mayor to speak and every one who had a seat sat down. Others stood in the warm May sunshine. In the third row just back from all the townspeople were Tanya and Bob, and Marjorie and Raymond Jordan. Angel had not seen Jake's parents since they arrived home, considering that they had only flown in the night before. They had been determined that they were not going to miss out on this grand occasion.

Angel and the girls stood off to one side. Arnold Brooks had been offered a seat but insisted that he stand quite near the front where he could see and hear everything. The rest of the seats available were occupied by whoever got there first. They were filled with family friends and curious onlookers from the town and neighbouring towns. There was also a surprising number of visitors from the city.

Angel had installed a guest book on the manor veranda, and she was looking forward to leafing through it later to see just where everyone had come from. But for now she was nervously fidgeting with the collar of her white jacket that she was finding a bit too warm. Underneath that she wore a black and white fitted linen dress, with a wide black belt and red shoes. She wore a large floppy hat on her head, which she found appropriate for the time, remembering her outfit when she'd first arrived at the manor nearly sixteen years ago.

Angel glanced over at the girls who stood beside her, both looking lovely. Mae was on her best behaviour, and Rachael seemed on guard, in case her mother needed anything. Her beautiful eyes darted across the crowd, making sure that everything was going as planned.

The mayor began his speech, and he was known to be a long-winded speaker. Angel was thinking about what she would say as she cut the ribbon to officially open Angel's Retreat, when she felt a hand slip into hers. She turned to see Bill Canton, and he was winking at her. Angel's eyes filled with tears, and she noticed immediately that she was not the only one with tear-filled eyes.

"What are you doing here?" she asked incredulously.

"Where else would I be?" he replied.

Angel stepped back from the rest and made a beeline for the back of the manor, she started down the path into the orchard and Bill was right behind her. Suddenly she stopped.

"I don't know what to make of you, Bill. But this is not a good time to show up."

"Hell, Angel, it took all my guts and courage to come, you know."

"And why would that be?"

"Because I have no right to expect you to forgive me."

"I can't get into this right now. I have a speech to make."

"I know. I'll just leave. Forget I ever came. Hell, forget you ever met me." He turned and started back for the manor.

"Bill, don't go."

Bill stopped in his tracks and wheeled around to face her. Anguish covered his face and sweat trickled off his brow. "I'm gonna make this fast. I came here to hope you'd forgive me and to tell you that I love you. Hell, I've loved you since the first day I saw you. My first thought that day was that some guys have all the luck, then guilt slid over me when I thought of Jake, and what he had lost and had to leave behind."

Angel stood like a statue. "You…love me?"

Bill rushed back to take her hands. "Of course I do, and I hope it's not too late to tell you that. I've been avoiding you simply because I do love you so much. I thought I was causing you nothing but trouble with the girls. Mae never would have taken off into the woods, if I hadn't been the cause of it. Hell, I've been the cause of all your misery lately, starting with Jake."

"You didn't make that accident happen, Bill." Tears were streaming down Angel's cheeks. "You were the reason I chose to live again. I want you in my life. The girls want you in their life. We've got a lot to talk about, but it can't be now."

"Mom, there you are." Rachael stood at the back of the manor. "Everyone is waiting for you to cut the ribbon. Come on."

Angel and Bill hurried up to meet her, and Rachael gave them both an encouraging smile.

As they rounded the corner, the mayor was just calling out Angel's name. In front of everyone, Bill grabbed Angel and kissed her. The crowd applauded and whether it was for the mayor's speech or the kiss, it was a loud uproar. Angel hardly heard any of it. She had been swept off to a place that she hadn't been since sixteen years ago, when Jake Jordan had first come into her life.

Lost in their own love and time, the mayor had to announce Angel's name three times before Rachael poked her mother and told her that she was being paged. Angel broke away from her entanglement with Bill's arms, and with a blush on her face and the warm afternoon breeze fanning her long red hair, she made her way to the podium.

EPILOGUE

One year after Angel's Retreat had been opened, Angel Jordan and William Canton, walked the deck of the catamaran and took their place at the bow of the boat. Family and friends gathered around, eagerly anticipating the day's event.

The morning had been cloudy and threatening, but as Angel had risen and gazed over the Bay of Fundy, she was not threatened by the weather. She was rather looking forward to the day, no matter what the weather held. All hands on deck, she thought, and if the rain did come, enough rain coats would be on board for the guests to shrug into. Nothing could put a damper on this day. It was her wedding day.

But Angel did not have to be concerned, because as the day wore on, the clouds dispersed and by afternoon with barely a cloud in the sky, Angel and Bill said their vows. It was an intimate port side ceremony with the peaceful sound of water lapping on the hull of the boat, and the scent of roses, apple blossoms and lilacs adorning every nook and cranny.

Rachael sat by her sister, Mae, and her Aunt Tanya and her Uncle Bob. Next to them were Rachael and Mae's grandparents, and Arnold Brooks and his daughter. Some of the guests were standing. Since Angel and Bill did not have any attendants, they stood alone in front of the minister. Standing guests included Bill's brother, Eric, and some of Angel and Bill's select friends. Bill's mother had of course been invited but had declined saying that boats made her nauseous.

Rachael grasped her little sister's hand as she noticed tears brimming in her eyes, but Mae wore a huge smile, and Rachael knew that they were tears of happiness. Their mother was getting married. It had been a long journey back from the tragic days of almost two years ago, when the girls had lost their beloved father. Rachael thought about the many sailing trips her family had taken, with her father at the helm of the boat. Now there would be a new captain.

She smiled to herself when she remembered the summer before. Although Bill had said he had a fair amount of sailing experience, she and Mae still had to teach him a few things about the catamaran. He was a fast learner however, and before long he was sailing like a pro. Now he and Angel would take the cat out into the Atlantic towards their honeymoon and first land stop at St. Andrews By-the-Sea in New Brunswick.

When the ceremony was complete, and the bride and groom walked down through the row of people with gleaming smiles on both their faces, glasses of champagne were raised to the exuberant couple. Mae held up a champagne glass of apple juice, even though she had complained earlier that she should be allowed to taste the champagne on such a special occasion.

The first one to step out of line was Arnold Brooks, as he congratulated the couple. "Here's to a long and happy union!"

"Here, here," Raymond Jordan spoke up next.

Marjorie Jordon, Jake's mother, stepped forward and gave Angel a hug. She whispered in her ear, "It's good to see you happy again, Angel. Jake would have wanted it this way."

Angel's eyes filled with tears. "Marjorie, I just know he's watching over us." She filled up so much, that she could not say another word, and Marjorie stepped back in line after patting her on the shoulder.

Eric stepped forward and gave his brother a man hug. "Good on yah, bro, you did good." Then he got closer and whispered, "She's a beauty."

"Don't I know it. Seems my luck has changed." Bill grinned at Eric. "Maybe someday you'll get lucky too."

"Mommy, I'm going to miss you." Mae hugged her mother so tight that Angel gasped. "Oh, Mae, you took my breath away. Now, you be on your best behaviour when you have to stay at Aunt Tanya's, okay?"

"I will, Mommy, and I get to stay at home with Rachael at night, don't I?"

"That's up to Rachael. If she plans to go out then you'll have to stay at Aunt Tanya's."

Mae made a face. "I'm old enough to stay alone."

"Mae, we've already discussed this before."

Mae shrugged, "Oh, okay. Have fun, Mommy." She moved back as others came forward to congratulate the bride and groom.

Rachael had been watching from a distances knowing she would have a special moment with her mother later, before they left. Right now she felt she should try and herd them all over to the *Captain's Cave* for the reception. Just as she was thinking about it, her aunt Tanya took over. Rachael decided to spend some time with her uncle who was sitting by himself in his wheelchair. Bob was not so good these days. He had good days and bad days and some really bad days, but today he seemed to be okay, so far.

****

As the wedding party made their way into the *Harbour Room*, which was a private area that overlooked the water and the sailboats, Angel and Bill stayed behind on the boat, while the photographer took a few pictures. Later, the three of them joined the rest, and the photographer did more pictures on the sun deck with a backdrop of the harbour.

The room was set up with an appropriate number of tables and the guest table for the bride and groom and Angel's two daughters. After the meal was complete, guests began to mingle, while staff removed the tables leaving an expansive dance floor area. A small band set up and it was time for the bride and the groom to have the first waltz. Rachael danced with Mae then changed partners when Eric came along. Raymond Jordan saw an opportunity to slip his arm around Mae and glide her across the floor.

The room was decorated much like the boat had been, with lots of roses in various colours and mounds of apple blossoms and lilacs that filled the room with intoxicating smells of spring.

After toasts were made round and round the room, it was time for Angel to break away. Rachael was watching and as soon as she saw her mother make an exit, she did the same. In a small room off the big room, Angel changed from her vanilla linen sheath into white deck pants and a white T-shirt that said, *Bride On Board*.

It was time to say goodbye. Rachael hugged her mother. "You two have an awesome time, you hear? And I don't want you to worry one bit about the retreat or Mae."

Angel blinked back tears. "I'm going to be lonesome. I haven't been away from Mae for this long ever."

"Mom, it's only two weeks."

Angel sniffed and dabbed at her eyes. "I know, I know, but that's a long time."

"Ah, you're going to be so busy with your new hubby that you won't have time to be lonesome. And he's turned out to be a pretty good sailor, otherwise, I'd never let you go with him."

Angel laughed. "I know a little about sailing myself, you know. It's just that when you guys are around, I don't bother."

"I know, Mom. You two will be fine. Just think, the first night of your honeymoon, out there with a gorgeous moon overhead. I'm so jealous."

"Your day will come, Rachael. And if you want to sail away on your honeymoon as well, then you'd better find a sailor."

"I'm looking, Mom, but I'm picky."

"You're like your dad, that's what he told me when we were driving to the Valley that first day I came to help Aunt May."

"Well, he picked a good one. I'm so forever grateful to have you in my life."

Just then Mae poked her head in the door. "So this is where you guys are."

Angel put her arms out. "Come here, baby. Come give your mom a goodbye kiss."

Mae wrapped her arms around her mother's waist and snuggled into her. "Have fun, Mommy. Lots of it. And bring lots of stuff back for us."

When Angel and the girls returned to the *Harbour Room*, all the guests had a good laugh at Angel's T-shirt. "Next thing we know," Arnold shouted, "you'll be wearin' one that says *Baby On Board.*"

Angel gave Bill a glance, and he was looking like the cat that ate the canary. "We'll have to see about that, Arnold. Who knows?"

The day was waning and clouds had gathered at the horizon. The sun shot a portrait of radiant colours up into the sky. By now Bill, who had been dressed in a lightweight, white suit, had removed the tie and jacket and rolled up his shirt sleeves. He linked his arm with Angel's and they said their goodbyes to the guests, who all ventured outside and down to the dock to watch the couple board the boat.

As they made their way out into the Bay of Fundy, the guests stood and watched. The sun was still visible in a red glow, the water shimmered with colour. The boat grew smaller and was now in full sail.

Rachael held her sister's hand as other members of the wedding party began to depart. Before long, only two small figures remained watching the sailboat turn into a tiny speck on the horizon. Darkness was settling in on shore and another wedding party was entering the restaurant, when Rachael and Mae walked to Rachael's car.

"I guess we did the right thing when we went to Bill's cabin last year."

"What else would we do?" Rachael asked her sister. "She's our mother and we wanted her to be happy."

"I bet Ralph is dying to pee," Mae said, changing the subject.

"Then we better get home." Rachael looked over at Mae. "If he does pee, you can clean it up, you're the one who volunteered to look after him."

Mae giggled. "But you're the veterinarian."

"Almost veterinarian," Rachael replied with a laugh, "and that doesn't matter, you're not getting out of doggie duties."

****

Angel stood by the helm with her arm around Bill's waist. She laid her head on his shoulder. "Are you happy with the day?"

"Happy is an understatement," Bill replied, snuggling her close to him. "Your idea to get married on the boat was a bit of brilliance, Angel. I think everyone enjoyed it."

"Oh, so I'm brilliant now."

"Yes...and indomitable."

Their laughter echoed over the bay as the sun slipped beneath the waves, leaving a scarlet blaze of glory in the night sky.

A Message from the Author

I hope you enjoyed reading Angel's Retreat as much as I enjoyed writing it. If you haven't already read Angel's Blessing, you might want to rejoin Angel in earlier times in her life.

The series I am working on now is The Dream Series. Book 1, 1964: Chasing a Dream and Book 2, Facing Reality are both available, and below I have inserted excerpts from each for your pre-reading pleasure. This winter I will be working on Book 3, Missing Link.

EXCERPT FROM 1964: CHASING A DREAM

Outside, a layer of heavy humidity blanketed the city. And although I wore a cool, sleeveless white blouse, cotton skirt and open sandals, I felt drenched. My cheeks were hot and my hair clung to my neck. I trudged up Canal Street, tucking the newspaper under my arm. The day loomed before me, long and arduous. I wished I were in Montgomery. At least I'd have Bobby's company. Memories, like approaching storms, smouldered, and from deep within the dark corners of my mind, an unknown void in my life seemed to take possession of me.

Suddenly, lightning scorched the sky through layers of low hanging purplish-grey clouds. Sheets of rain cataracted to the pavement. Thankful for my newspaper, I used it as a shield over my head to ward off the assaulting raindrops. Hurrying now, I turned into the French Quarter. Pedestrians speedily vacated the streets, which were dismal and depressing. Finally, shaking with dampness, I rushed through an open doorway. Smells of food and strains of classical music greeted me. Tossing the paper on a table, I dropped into a chair and looked around while lighting up a smoke. It was an ancient-looking place with peeling walls and splintery, dark wood. I smiled at the dark-haired waiter, who stood over me with a menu in hand.

"Oh, I'm not hungry," I told him. "Just wet."

"Yes, but are you dry inside? How about a drink to lift your spirits?" He winked.

"Well, I could use it, I suppose. What is this place?"

"This is Napoleon House." He smiled, showing bright, gleaming teeth. His black hair was slicked back, looking wet, as if he'd just been caught in the downpour too. "May I suggest Pimm's Cup?" I looked at him blankly. "Your drink," he said.

"Oh, yes. Okay." He took the menu and moved away. I looked around the room again. The bar was full, and a blonde lady near the end laughed and chatted with a black-haired man, who sported a heavy moustache. His bushy eyebrows danced as he told her a story.

Next to them, two long-haired men looked dazed as they raised tall glasses in unison. My waiter returned with a cool-looking drink, topped with a cucumber slice. "Enjoy." He smiled. "Just snap at me if there's anything else."

"Snap at you?"

He grinned and walked away snapping his fingers. I sighed. Sometimes I felt so stupid. I was okay when out with Joe, but on my own I was lost. I sipped the refreshing drink and was soon joined by one of the long-haired men from the bar. "You alone?" he said, placing his glass on the table. He sat across from me looking dismal.

I shuddered then decided I was safe enough in the company of so many people. "Yes, I'm alone. I just ducked in from the rain. This seems like a nice place."

"Yes. I come here a lot," he replied.

"Really. Why?"

"I like the ambiance."

"Oh? Well it is rather mellow and relaxing. The drinks are good too." I snapped my fingers and my waiter came quickly. "How about another one?" I asked, smiling at him.

"What do you do?" the long-haired man asked.

I laughed. "That's a very good question. I'm presently looking for work."

He smiled, then I noticed when he wasn't looking glum he looked quite nice. His eyes were a warm, grey shade, and his mouth had a sensuous bow shape.

"I'm a writer," he volunteered. "I get my inspirations from the music and the ambiance."

His eyes took on a sparkle, and he pulled a small notebook from his shirt pocket. Flipping the pages, he settled on one and placed the book in front of me. "It's blank," I announced, looking into his grey eyes.

"Of course. Then write."

"Oh, I can't. You write." I shoved the book towards him.

He shoved it back. "Think. Listen to the music, and feel thee—"

"The ambiance?" I grinned and we both laughed.

I stared at the blue-lined page then looked up. He was staring at me, holding out a pen. Gingerly, I accepted it and looked around the room once more. No inspiration. What did he expect? But he continued to sit quietly, staring now into his drink. I sipped my own and gazed through the open doorway. My eyes grew heavy as the splatters of rain, beating rhythmically on the pavement, created a hypnotic trance. *Dream Killer.* The words screamed in my head.

"Dream Killer," I announced.

My friend flashed his eyes at me, as I hurriedly wrote the title on the blue-lined page. Words tumbled over one another like they couldn't get out of my head fast enough and onto the blank page. When I finished, I sat back and sighed. Then reaching for my half-empty glass, I looked at him.

"Well?" he asked, seemingly holding his breath. I pushed the notebook across the table, and he snatched it up and scanned the page, while I sipped my drink. A broad grin formed across his face. "You must read," he said. "Justin," he called to his friend at the bar. "There's going to be a reading."

"No," I protested. "I can't do that." Justin joined us and read my poem.

"Yes, you must read," he insisted.

"No, I won't," I said. "I can't do it."

Justin turned to my friend. "Then you read, Lee."

Lee looked at me dumbfounded. "Should I?"

I shrugged. "Do you want to?"

"I will," he declared eagerly, picking up the notebook.

Justin walked towards the bar and moved along the line of seated patrons, speaking with each one as he passed. Then at the corner of the bar, he took a stool and reached behind the counter for a mike. Holding it close to his mouth he boomed, "My fellow comrades, your attention, please."

Everyone turned to face him, and the room was so quiet only the rhythmic rain and accompanying background music could be heard.

"Today my comrade, Lee, will read from the pen of..." He looked anxiously around the room, his eyes finally settling on mine. Suddenly all eyes were turned my way. Each pair questioning my response.

Lee, who was still standing beside me clutching the notebook, nudged me. "Your name, he doesn't know your name," he whispered fervently.

I jumped up, the noise from the chair legs squeaked under me. "Marlee Sweet," I proclaimed, in a voice louder than I knew I owned. All eyes scanned me momentarily, and I shrank back on my chair. When I got the courage to look up again, Lee was replacing Justin on the stool. With mike in hand and a rain-soaked musical backdrop, he cleared his throat and began:

DREAM KILLER

Dismal deadwood in my head, crawling cockroaches in my bed.
Moments of splendour between the sheets, foolish hopes and dreams.
Run away, you runaway. Hide your face in shame. All fall down and
Then repeat – over again.
Dismal deadwood, all chopped up, cockroach crushed by heavy cup.
Dazzling sheets fly on clothesline, put the dreams away.
Locked in boxes out of sight, open them and dreams take flight.
Run about collecting them to store away again.
Sun is shining, let it in. Open windows, doors and heart.
All fall down and then repeat— over again.
Dreams collected, gathered up, mixed with cockroach in a cup.
Never again to be the same. Bittersweet, all dreams that wear your name.

He bowed his head, and a thunderous applause blocked out the music and the rain from the street. I couldn't believe they were applauding my poem, or was it the reader? Lee returned to my table, and the crowd returned to their drinks and chatter. The rain and music resumed, and I ordered another Pimm's Cup, accompanied by a muffuletta sandwich.

Lee, sitting across from me, ripped the page from his notebook, folded it and handed it to me. "It's good, Marlee. I'm honoured to have read it."

"You actually mean that?" I said. "It's just a bunch of words. I don't even know where it came from."

"From the music and the ambiance," he said, grinning.

My drink and food arrived, and Lee said he had to leave. At the door both Lee and Justin waved goodbye. After I finished, I ventured outside. The rain was a steady drizzle. I clutched the sodden newspaper in my hand and let the raindrops settle on my head and descend over my body, drenching my clothes until they stuck to me. I walked home surrounded by the hazy afternoon, and the memories of the free spirits I had met in Napoleon House. My poem, folded and dry, was tucked securely inside my purse.

By the time I reached my street, the sky had lightened and a thread of sunlight spun through an opening in the overcast, settling like a warm, friendly arm across my shoulder.

EXCERPT FROM FACING REALITY

The press was now referring to our group as *Marlee and the B Band*. That didn't impress Byron. He was reading a review one night at my place, as all the guys had started hanging out there again. "Jesus Christ, they changed the name. Sonofabitch."

We all gathered around to look at the paper. We looked at each other and sort of grinned, but we knew Byron wasn't happy, not at all.

But the name stuck and he reluctantly went along with it. We were doing pretty well then, and we didn't need any set-backs. If that's what the press wanted to call us, Byron knew he couldn't make waves. Whether he liked it or not, I was the feature of his band.

One Saturday night after we got back from out of town, Byron hung around my place after the other guys had gone home. I was tired and said to him, "Good night, Byron, see you in a couple of days. I'm gonna sleep them away." Byron didn't make any move to leave so I encouraged him. I said, "Good night, Byron, don't you have a home?"

That's when he mumbled, "No."

"What? What's going on?"

"I got kicked out of my place."

"When?"

"Last week before we went out of town. All my stuff is at Jake's."

"Okay, what happened?"

He told me a long sob story about getting behind in his rent and apparently owing everyone money.

"Byron, you make a lot of money, what are you doing with it?" He rolled up his sleeve and showed me the needle marks. I was disgusted. "Damn it, Byron, you should have more sense."

"Listen who's talking. You're no princess in white. Bungled up a record deal cause you couldn't stay sober."

"So what?" I retaliated. "At least I pay my bills. Well, you might as well stay here tonight." I went to the closet and got him a blanket and a pillow. I tossed them at him and told him to use the sofa. That was the beginning of my relationship with Byron. He wasn't always at my place, but he was there a good deal of the time. And on days and nights when we didn't have a gig, we would get strung out together.

Sometimes Byron would play his guitar and we would sing. One night he started singing a song I didn't know, and I thought it was beautiful. It was my type of song, lonely and wistful. I asked him about it and he said he'd written it. He sang it for me once more. It was called *Make Me Love You*. Byron's deep voice seemed to tremble as he sang the lyrics.

Make me love you like I know you can
Do it kindly and I'll be your man
Make me feel the love that only lives in a dream…
In a dream…
I've been watching you from far away
Wondering what it might be like someday
Make me love you like I know you can
Do it gently and I'll be your man…

Byron stopped abruptly and put his guitar down. He reached for me and kissed me. I was lonely and starved for love. As he started undoing the buttons on my shirt, I kissed him with passion I'd thought I'd buried in the past.

He was like no one else. He wasn't gentle and patient. His kisses were wild and rough. It was almost to the point of pain. I descended into a dark ocean of feeling. All at once he changed. He whispered to me, "Do it gently and I'll be your man."

Somehow I knew what he wanted. I caressed him and kissed him gently. I tried to be so tender, everything had changed. He loved tenderness but he didn't know how to give it. I held him back and helped him to be patient. Slowly we made love and it was tender and precious.

After that night, Byron and I spent a lot of time together. We never slept together on the road and we tried to keep our private and public lives separate, but after a while things got muddled up and we couldn't keep the two apart anymore. I hated being alone at that time and when Byron would shoot drugs, I would get a bottle and drink until I could join him on his level.

One night we sat on the floor in my apartment with our backs to the wall. We were getting high, and I was thinking about Byron's song and I said out loud, "It's about me isn't it?"

"What's about you, Coppertop?"

"The song, *Make Me Love you.*"

"Guess again," Byron answered.

"Come on, Byron, do it gently and I'll be your man? I've been watching you from far away? It is isn't it?"

"So, what if it is?"

"Why, Byron, I never knew you cared. You were always so sarcastic to me, so moody and angry."

"I don't like you, okay? But I lust for you. I want to fuck you all the time."

He made a lunge forward and grabbed for me. I leaned to the left and he fell on my shoulder.

"You're pitiful, you know that?" I spat at him.

"Me, pitiful? You're the one's pitiful. You think I don't know you're carrying a torch? Moaning out those love songs. Whoever he is, you've got it bad."

"So what, Byron? You like to see people in pain? I don't suppose you've ever been in love."

"I told you before it's goddamn horse shit."

Byron and I went on that way, while the summer turned into fall. We hated each other, while we lusted for the other's body. Most of the time, when we weren't on the road, we just stayed in the apartment getting high. But when we made love, it came out right. We were a volatile combination. I would take the phone off the hook for days and never even answer the door. I was hurting, we both were. And we consoled each other in the only way we knew how.

One night, while I was looking for something, I accidentally hung the phone up. It had been on the floor amongst a pile of clothing. All at once it rang. Stunned as I was in an alcoholic haze, I picked it up and said hello.

"Marlee, thank God I finally reached you."

"Who is this?"

"It's Grace. I have bad news, dear. Dad passed away yesterday."

"What?" I strained to comprehend what I was hearing.

"I've tried to call you before but your line has been busy or something. Marlee, are you there?"

"Yes, yes I am. How's Mom?" It was all I could think about.

"She's sedated. The funeral's tomorrow at four. Do you think you could make it? If you can get a flight, someone can meet you at the airport."

I couldn't think of seeing Dad in a casket so I took the coward's way out. "I don't know. I'll have to call you back. I have to check the airlines."

I hung up the phone then I waited awhile and called Grace back. "I'm sorry, Grace, I can't get a flight." She was disappointed but she said she would explain things to Mom and Rose.

I never even tried to get a flight out. I had lied to Grace. I couldn't face any of them. I sat in the dark and thought about Dad and our conversation before he left for Nova Scotia.

Don't ever give up your dreams, he had said, or something like that. I decided right then that I was going to shape up and get my life back together. I wanted to make it in this business. I'd do it for Dad. I switched on a light and looked at a calendar. I was trying to understand what date it was and when Dad had died.

"Let's see," I mumbled. "This is the thirteenth, he died yesterday the twelfth....the twelfth," I repeated, and something didn't seem right. I started going back on the calendar and counting up the days, but it wasn't about Dad. It was about my cycle. I realized I was three weeks past my period.

15630446R00091

Printed in Great Britain
by Amazon